Helen Mathers

Cherry Ripe!

A Romance - Vol. 1

Helen Mathers

Cherry Ripe!
A Romance - Vol. 1

ISBN/EAN: 9783337351021

Printed in Europe, USA, Canada, Australia, Japan

Cover: Foto ©Andreas Hilbeck / pixelio.de

More available books at **www.hansebooks.com**

A Romance.

BY THE AUTHOR OF

"COMIN' THRO' THE RYE," "THE TOKEN OF THE
SILVER LILY."

"Could ye come back to me, Douglas, Douglas,
In the old likeness that I knew,
I could be so loving, so tender and true,
Douglas, Douglas, tender and true."

IN THREE VOLUMES.

VOL. I.

Third Edition.

LONDON:
RICHARD BENTLEY AND SON,
1878.

"CHERRY RIPE!"

BOOK I.
BLOSSOM.

CHAPTER I.

" Just so may love, although 'tis understood
The mere commingling of passionate breath,
Produce more than our searching witnesseth."

" FUN !" said Mignon.

" This way !" cried Lu-Lu.

Fate, choosing so insignificant a means as the fact of two girls running away from their governess, to alter the current of four persons' lives, directed their steps to the left instead of to the right, and sent them spinning round one of the big trees of

the avenue with such velocity, that a gentleman, who was advancing slowly from the
opposite direction, found himself all at once
deprived of breath, hat, stick, and patience.

"Upon my word!" said he angrily, and
for the moment too much astonished at the
hearty and simultaneous onslaught on his
person, to be at all sure of the sex of his
assailants.

"I *beg* your pardon!" said Lu-Lu.

Glancing sharply at the apple-cheeked,
black-eyed schoolgirl, the young man discovered in her face no reason why he should
set aside the bad temper and *ennui* that de-
voured him, to assure her of his gratitude for
the favour just accorded.

"We are *very* sorry!" said Mignon; and
then he turned suddenly, and saw before him
something that all his life long he thought he
must have been seeking, yet had never until
now found; discovered a want that in all its
depth and fulness he had never known until
in this, its moment of fulfilment; felt that here
at least was something by no means to be

included in the bitter, weary disgust for himself, the world, and all within it, that this day filled his stormy, passionate soul to overflowing.

> " And soon his eyes had drunk her beauty up,·
> Leaving no drop in the bewildering cup,
> And still the cup was full . . . ."

And in that moment was the wheel of his life's fate and hers set moving, and the end thereof, how could he tell it any more than the girl who stood facing him beneath the pink and white blossoms of the flowering chestnuts, with something of the wonder and puzzle of the young May morning in her innocent, childish eyes ?

" We are very sorry," she said again gently, thinking how terribly put out he seemed to be about no such great matter, and not daring to smile for fear of making him yet more angry.

He almost laughed aloud as it suddenly flashed through his mind, what a pity it was that none of his friends were by, to see the ridiculous figure he cut before this pair of schoolgirls. The gay words that would at any other time have sprung quick as lightning to his lips; the bold devil-may-care spirit that would instantly have turned the ludicrous mischance to at least the semblance of a *bonne aventure*—where were they now? and what magic was this that stole the wit from his brain, the words from his tongue, and the power to do aught save stand looking—looking—at the girl before him?

The matter—it had in all occupied not more than thirty seconds—was cut short by an act on the part of the culprits, that proved them to be no embryo fine ladies with fashionable notions of their own importance, for Mignon fetched his hat, Lu-Lu picked up his stick; and, having placed his property in his hands, they dropped him the simplest, sweetest, prettiest courtesy in the world, apiece, moved quickly away, and vanished.

Their disappearance broke the spell; he put on his hat, turned about, and followed them.

That they were bent on mischief of some kind was pretty clear, seeing how they tacked this way and that, avoiding the open, and casting so many glances to the right and left, as could not fail, he thought, to discover him sooner or later to their eyes. Only it so happened that they were not thinking of him just then, no, nor of any other young man, nor of anything in the whole world but to get away all by themselves, to enjoy the full freshness and glory of this peerless spring morning, to revel in the rosy feast of blossom that hung overhead . . . and this, they were so dainty and delicate in their fancies as to imagine they could not do, under the guardianship of mademoiselle, and in the company of the dozen or so of noisy hoydenish pupils placed under her charge. And if it should appear strange that two schoolgirls could be found, who were not moved to foolish smiles and *minauderies* by the mere sight and neighbourhood of a young and handsome man, I am bound to confess that these were altogether exceptional maidens, and, both by training and habit of thought, had preserved intact an innocence of mind more usually to be met with in misses of eight or ten than of

sixteen and seventeen. That they had enjoyed a hearty laugh at his expense as soon
as they were safely out of earshot, is not to
be denied; or that when, later, they perceived him close at hand, they looked at one
another with a certain air of particularity that
betokened the existence of a latent understanding between them; but that they were
guiltless of either giggle or undue excitement
he was careful to note, being a man of most
fastidious taste, and quick to observe the
smallest sign of levity in woman.

Afterwards, when he tried to remember
how he spent that day, he was not able : save
that he was sure he had sat under the trees
for a long while; and he thought he had
eaten bread and butter, and chocolate, and
Turkish Delight—but no, he could not have
done that, it must have been somebody else;
that he had looked at a great many pictures,
and heard a great many criticisms passed on
them by a pair of merciless young judges,
one of whom in her bloom and brightness
eclipsed whatever she regarded; that he had

gone on a wild-goose chase in and out, and
round and about the Maze, following one
little pair of feet that seemed to know no
flagging; that he had fed one of the big
white swans that came sailing proudly down
the mimic lake with a little lovely cygnet
perched high upon its wings—to his dying
day he never forgot that little creature, or how
its whiteness showed like snow against its
mother, that was fair enough when it stood
alone, God knows. He also had a distinct
impression that three or four times he had
been all but caught and held in durance vile
by a sallow-faced Frenchwoman, but had each
time escaped by the skin of his teeth . . . .
and yet that could not have been himself, but
the girl whose shadow he was that day, and
whose name was Mignon. He was quite
sure of that, for had he not heard her so
called by Lu-Lu many times that day? also
that she lived at Rosemary, Lilytown, for
which place had he not five minutes ago seen
her set out, seated in a great open van
drawn by two stout cart-horses? From the

stolid, bumpkinish Jehu, who was a curiosity
indeed to be found within ten miles of
London town, he had by golden means, and
quite unobserved, as he thought, extracted
this latter information concerning her place
of abode.

Nor could he remember in the days that
came afterwards, at what time she went
away, and whether it were afternoon or
evening ; he only knew that it was daylight,
and the sky still blue overhead, when he
turned back, and threw himself down under
one of the giant trees of the avenue, to think.
About when he had first met her he was
more certain ; it was quite early, ten o'clock
perhaps ; this he knew, because all his life
long he could never see a young, exquisitely
fresh May morning without the girl's face
coming up before him. Mignon . . . . that
was her name, fanciful, tender, and un-
English, yet one that became her curiously
well, he thought . . . . and then he fell to
watching the rose and white leaves of the
chestnut flowers come fluttering slowly down;

observed how the glisten of the sun caught
the inner side of one of the big prickly leaves,
turning it to gold; discovered how enchanting
was the tiny patch of blue overhead, that the
envious boughs had failed to altogether shut
out from the daisies and grass that loved it
. . . . and the snow and the red of the
vagrant petals, the liquid gold of the sun-
touched leaf, the bit of bright blue tapestry
above, wove themselves unconsciously into a
fairy likeness of a girl's face. . . . For were
they not all there—the tints of her skin, the
colour of her hair, the very hue of her eyes?
But the look that had caught and fixed his
regard, and upon which his heart had closed,
he found not in either blossom, or leaf, or
sky, for it sprang direct from that purest of
all sources, a maiden's innocent soul; and
because his own life was just then so full of
strife, and sin, and misery, this same look of
hers outweighed in his eyes the mere beauty
that many a time he had seen possessed by
women in a far higher degree. Mignon . . . .
what fate did her name foretell, and what did

her face say ? It could be nothing to him, this future of hers, for was not his own lot in life fixed, the stage prepared, the last act but one in a reckless, unhappy, and guilty past about to be played out ?

A bird came whirling into a cluster of the stately blooms overhead, and as the dainty column swayed under his eager, slender feet, he poured out a sweet gay song of gladness, that was his tribute of gratefulness for his happy life, his beautiful mate, his long summer day of sunshine, and love, and plenty. And the song of the bird, and the peace and beauty of the evening and the hour, stole into the man's heart, until he knew it not for that which had beat in his breast no longer ago than this morning . . . . Hither he had come in a mood of black and impious rebellion against all things in heaven and earth. With eyes turned inwards, he had passed all outward things by, nor observed any one of the tender and manifold surprises of the morning, though, if any one had asked him, he would have answered,

" *Yes, it is a fine May morning, and the
chestnuts are in bloom;*" but the *heart* of the
man was dead to Nature's teaching, as it had
been for many long years—ay, ever since he
had taken to reading and playing upon the
vices, faults, and weaknesses of the men and
women who came in his path.

Whence, then, came to him, in a breath,
this clearness of the eyes, this subtle understanding of all that was fair and gracious,
this capacity for drawing into some new and
fragrant chamber of the soul, aught so
evanescent, so impalpable, so delicate, as the
quivering light on a leaf, the shifting colour
of the sky, or the painting of a flower that
had passed through the hands of the Creator ?

Thoughts unwonted and gentle came to
him there . . . . of his dead mother ; she
had not been in his memory this half-dozen
years or more . . . . recollections of his
boyhood, and the eager bright days of his
youth, when existence had seemed to him
but a cup filled to the brim with a cunning
and rarely-mingled draught of sweetness, of

which he could not drink too often, or too
deeply . . . . to-night he found himself able
to look back upon that time with none of the
scorn and pity with which he had in these
latter days grown to regard that hopeful and
not unworthy period of his life ; nay, some of
the old keen flavour and enjoyment of it
seemed to be once more between his lips as
he lay and mused, and dreamed, and thought
. . . . some new influence was upon him,
gentle and humanising, to-night, and blame
him not that in yielding to it, he perceived
not how that which appeared to him as the
touch of an angel's wing was in very truth
a snare set for him by Satan, nor knew that
in this, his awakening to all things good and
lovely, he had never been tempted to so black
a sin, so foul a wrong as now.

This morning when he had walked forth,
his worldly callous heart full to the brim
with bitterness and revolt, he had yet been
a better, more honest man than now, when
the very means that awakened his heart to
the recognition of beauty in goodness, and

goodness in beauty, took its root in a half-conceived dishonour that had in it all the elements of crime, in the shadow cast before of a deed that would stamp the doer as a recreant to all those traditions of honour that no man may traverse without inflicting a stain upon his character that, in his own eyes at least, can never be wiped away.

Has one ever paused to note how that pure and stainless flower the waterlily grows? From filth and slime and every conceivable noisomeness she springs, to crown the bosom of the waters with her snowy cup; and among us all is there one so cunning that he can tell by what wondrous alchemy the vileness is transmuted to beauty, the uncleanliness to unsullied purity, the very nadir of degradation to the perfection of an unsurpassable splendour?

And even as this lily grows, borrowing her purity we know not whence, her beauty we know not how, so may it not be that from the dark unkindly soil of a sinful human heart, may be born a passion that, while having its root in foulness, and owing its very existence to shame and transgression, shall grow to a vigorous stately flower, that, in the beholding, we are almost fain to forget whence it has arisen ?

For as from richest and most healthful soil, with every favouring influence of sunshine, wind, and rain, may creep into life a noxious deadly poison, a thing of hatefulness, whence our eyes turn with fear and loathing, so is it not given to us to say, " By such and such means was the evil turned to good, and the good to evil ;" we can but blindly puzzle out a meaning for ourselves, nor dare to lift our brows to Heaven and, with boasting pride, cry aloud that we have found it.

Only this is certain, that the man into whose heart that day had sunk a germ, potential of life, form, and variation, that was by the inevitable law of progression bound to fulfil itself, and who had by sin fallen from his high estate, by sin alone, and the virtue that took its birth from that sin, was lifted again to it . . . . and that as he

would to his life's end have been guiltless of
his crowning infamy had not a girl's face that
day crossed his path, so would he have lived
and died with soul unawakened to good, so
would he never have raised his eyes to those
heights of greatness and self-mastery, to
which he, all sinning, humbled, and despairing, yet dared to aspire—ay, and by the
grace of God to reach at last.

CHAPTER II.

"Clear summer has forth walked
Unto the clover sward, and she has talked
Full soothingly to every mated finch."

THERE floated over the wall so joyful and exquisite a peal of laughter, that a young man, who was walking in the garden on the other side, was seized with some such curiosity as once set a certain old King pulling up his slippers, and putting on his spectacles, when he spied the unusual crowd collected in the royal pigsty, on the occasion of his naughty princess kissing the swineherd.

Mr. Babbage informs us that " the air is one vast library, in whose pages are for ever written all that man said and woman whispered;" but he does not tell us what becomes of the laughter so plentifully cast upon it day by day, and that surely has a character of its own, jocund, bitter, false, despairing, and is as much the language of the heart as words or tears, though we could fancy that some such mirth as that just uttered might sound sweet and pleasant after the lapse of more than one century.

It suggested all manner of sunshiny humorous things, as of a witty jest, a consummately ludicrous situation, a strikingly happy thought, or any one of those absurdities that provoke poor toiling human nature to amusement, and are in themselves a species of luxury.

"I wonder what she is laughing at now?" said he who listened, smiling to himself for company. "I have a very good mind to find out," he added aloud (for there was nobody by, not even a blackbird, to hear him).

He paused in his walk, and looked upwards.

At the top of the wall, flourishing hardily and sweetly, grew a tough little colony of wallflowers that had grown, the wind and the rain only knew how, and had come, the birds of the air only knew whence, affording, as he was well aware, a moderate screen from behind which a discreet person might peep without much chance of being detected.

Hard by, a ladder leaned against a peach-tree with a rakish air, as though it had given over work for the day, and was enjoying itself. This he fetched, pitched exactly opposite the wallflower, and proceeded to mount the same with as bold and unfaltering a step, as though spying into a neighbour's garden were the most ordinary thing in the world, and no more reprehensible than over-looking an opponent's hand at whist, or reading a letter backwards, or any other of those dishonourable little actions by which we deceive our friends, and open our eyes to our own delinquencies.

He mounted the first dozen or so of rungs

boldly, but slackened his pace as he rose higher, for ever so small an excess of courage or indiscretion might cause him to be discovered in a position that no young man would, to say the least, be proud to fill.

Therefore, albeit he was no faint-hearted person, he could not but feel it to be rather an awful moment when he topped the wall, and, pushing aside the scanty leaves and stalks of the wallflowers, gazed down into the garden some twenty feet below him.

The sight that met his eyes was curious but pretty, not particularly laughable in itself, yet tickling the beholder with a certain sense of pleasure that served all the purposes of laughter without demanding the outward expression of it : the subtlest and keenest enjoyment is, oftener than not, voiceless.

Seated in her coach, with skirts tucked well up around her, and two little neatly-shod feet and ankles full in view, sat a very young lady. Her coachman did not precede, but was behind her, horses she had none, and although she rode with a hand extended on either side and as majestic an air as though she were seated in the Lord Mayor's own on the 9th of November, Mignon's coach was, I am bound to confess, no more and no less than a wheel-barrow. She had a white pocket-handkerchief tied over her head, and the richest of red roses were blooming in her beautiful young cheeks as she came whirling past the peeper.

" Faster ! faster !" she cried ; " do you not know that Gretna Green is yet three miles away, and that I have a most particular appointment, with a most particular person, to keep at half-past four *precisely ?*"

For answer, there came a whirr ! whiff ! and off flew the solitary wheel of Mignon's chariot, seating her with considerable emphasis on the exact centre of a parsley bed, that flourished greenly below the wall-flowers.

" There !" she cried ; and her voice was so young, and fresh, and gay, as to communicate to the listener a delightful sensation of novelty and enjoyment, as when one hears

> " A noise like of a hidden brook
>   In the leafy month of June,
> That to the sleeping woods all night
>   Singeth a quiet tune."

" I always *knew* that would happen one of these days, and if I were a fine woman like you, Prue, it would have happened *long* ago !"

" Well, Miss Mignon," said Prue, sitting down on a three-legged stool, with her back to the wall, and drawing some needlework from her pocket, " I'm not so sorry neither, for in my 'pinion riding in a barrow ain't the suitablest thing for a young lady like you."

" Nevertheless," said the girl, regarding her prone chariot regretfully, " I should never get half as much fun out of a coach and six as I've done out of that old piece of wood— not that I'm ever likely to possess a coach and *one !*"

"I'm none so sure of that," said Prue, nodding sagaciously. "Just you have a little patience, and you'll see what you *will* see."

"The days of Cinderella are over," said the girl, laughing and shaking her *blonde* head; "and all the fairy princes are asleep or bewitched, though even if they were awake and about, they would not be likely to trouble themselves to look for a little insignificant school-girl like me! Why, except Bumble, and one other person, and you, I don't believe there's a soul who cares whether I'm dead or alive!"

"It do seem a cruel shame," said Prue frowning; "if you was a foundling so to speak, you couldn't be worse off than you are for friends and folks of your own."

"I have got *her*," said the girl gaily; "or at least I shall have her very soon, for at any hour—any minute she may walk in, and then what a time we will have of it—she and I, and you, together!"

Prue, compressing her lips tightly, shook her head, but made no remark.

"But until she comes," resumed Mignon, "there is no denying the fact that our existence here is—dull! Now I wonder if there is any bit of mischief about that a tolerably well brought up young woman could possibly get herself into? If my gowns were smart enough—which they're *not*" (she spread out her skirt with both hands and regarded it ruefully), "we might go to the Park and look at all the fine people, but as it is, we have only Hampton Court and Madame Tussaud's to choose from, and I know both of *them* by heart!"

"Miss Sorel said we might go to the Poly — something, where they improve folk's morals—" began Prue.

"But I don't want my morals improved," said the girl. "I want to be amused, and—and oh! Prue, will you *ever* forget the last time we went to Hampton Court?"

"That was a very rum—I beg pardon, miss — a very *peculiar* go," said Prue,

grinning and looking disdainful. " If Miss
Sorel had been at home, it never would have
happened, but there, them furrineering mam-
selles don't know nothing !"

"Shall I ever get it out of my head?"
cried the girl, breaking into sudden laughter.

> " 'Four and twenty blackbirds
>   Baked in a pie,'

only *we* were baked in a van ! We must
have looked fine when we drove from the
door, every alternate girl visible through the
open framework at the sides, like a saint in a
niche with her back to the congregation,
bounding, jumping, jolting, creaking, bones
rattling, lockets dancing, teeth chattering—
was there ever such a shaking up upon
earth ? We were black and blue next day,
Prue !"

" I'll tell Miss Sorel when she comes back,"
said Prue with decision.

" Though, after all," said Mignon, "it was
a charming day—all but for one thing, and
that was dreadful !"

" What was that, miss ?" said Prue, looking
up quickly.

" Miss Lu-Lu and I nearly knocked down
—a man !" said Mignon ; " worse than that
—a *young* man ! If we had beaten him with
sticks," she went on, looking thoughtfully at
the two pretty feet placed in the first position
before her, " he could not have looked more
astonished and nonplussed !"

" How did it happen, miss ?" said Prue,
regarding her mistress with covert but keen
inquiry, and pausing in her work.

" We were running away from mademoiselle
and the girls," said Mignon, " and, alas ! just
as we spun round one of the big trees of the
avenue, she one side, I the other, we caught
a gentleman who was advancing two simultaneous blows, one on the right shoulder, the
other on the left—for a moment I do believe
he thought he saw *double !*"

" Did he *speak*, miss ?" inquired Prue with
interest.

" No indeed," said Mignon, laughing, " that
he did not ! Although we begged his pardon

twice over, and even picked up the property
of which our onslaught had deprived him, he
never uttered one syllable! It occurred to
us afterwards that perhaps the poor man was
dumb!"

" Dumb?" repeated Prue in an accent of
incredulity ; " dumb did you say, miss? Ho !
ho ! ho ! I beg pardon, miss, but—Ho ! ho !
ho ! ho !"

Mignon looked in astonishment at the
woman, who seemed to be struggling against
a grotesque and secret merriment, that
mastered her against her will.

" And pray," said the young lady with
dignity, " is it such a very *odd* thing, that a
man should be dumb? Hundreds of people
are—and blind as well—and they all marry,
and have deaf and dumb families !"

" I daresay, miss," said Prue, recovering,
" but somehow the notion tickled my fancy,"
and here she showed symptoms of a relapse
—" but can you mind what he was like, Miss
Mignon ?"

" Very dark—with very blue eyes, an

Irish combination that's too *womanish* I think for a man! And perhaps because we had been so rude to *him*," she went on, leaning her fair head against the wall, "he thought he would be rude to *us*, for he followed us about the whole day, and even came to see us set off in the van! And Miss Sorel always tells us that it is a very great insult for a gentleman with whom one is not acquainted to stare at and walk behind one."

"So it is, miss," said Prue, "generally."

"And yet," said Mignon meditatively, "it is not considered a rude thing for a young man to fall in love with a person—quite the reverse! You see he must make a beginning somewhere, and really it is rather difficult to say where rudeness ends, and politeness begins."

"What put that notion into your head, miss?" said Prue, looking sharply at the girl.

"Ah!" said Mignon, "that's a secret. Heigho!" she sighed, "how I wish something would happen—just to brisk us up, and set us going—if somebody would only take the trouble to write me a letter even, I think I could be satisfied !"

" A letter ?" said Prue, starting, " and who'd be after writing to you, but Miss Lu-Lu, or Miss Sorel, dear heart ? And you heard from both of *them* last week."

" There is nobody else," said Mignon ; " *she* would not write, she would come. But all the same I should love to have a letter— from *anybody*, I don't care who—just to make me feel that I was not such a terribly unimportant little person—that there was one person at least in the world to trouble her head about me !"

Something in Prue's pocket, as the money of spendthrifts is historically supposed to do, suddenly burnt her, and as she looked at the wistful, lovely face, that made the sunshine and happiness of her life, she cast all scruples and hesitation to the winds, and, taking off her thimble and laying down her work with sudden decision :

"Supposing, miss," she said, "that there *was* people in the world to trouble their heads to think about you, and supposing that 'twasn't a HER at all, but a HIM, why, what then, Miss Mignon?"

CHAPTER III.

"While every eve saw me my hair up-tying
  With fingers cool as aspen leaves . . . .
  I was as vague as solitary dove,
  Nor knew that nests were built."

 "A HIM?" said Mignon, laughing gaily, "but I don't know a single one who is likely to do anything of the sort!"

"Hasn't it ever struck you, Miss Mignon, that maybe, one of these days, you'd be picking up a *beau?*"

"No," said Mignon, clasping her arms round her knees, and leaning her head so far back that the wallflower got an excellent view of a pretty, straight nose, and some long brown eyelashes. "I can't say it ever has, Prue. It is not often that a schoolgirl arrives at the dignity of a real *beau!* Though indeed," she added, sighing, "it must be a *charming* thing, Prue, when once one has got used to it! Tell me, did you ever have one like that—all to your own self?"

"Maybe," said Prue, turning a handsome brick-dust colour, "but that was a long time ago, Miss Mignon."

"And were you in love with him?"

"No, miss, I never would—for fear. Falling in love's a ticklish thing—very."

"Did he ever write to you?" inquired Mignon, surveying Prue with positive respect, and from a totally new point of view, "because if he did, and if you would not mind it very much, I should so *like* to read one of his letters! I never read a *real* love-letter in all my life, and for a particular reason that I can't explain to you just now, I am so *anxious* to see *how it's done!*"

Prue, looking anxiously at her young mistress, plaited and unplaited her apron with restless, clumsy fingers. A struggle

of some kind was evidently going forward
in her mind. . . . She was but an ignorant,
gentle-hearted woman, who ardently desired
to act for the good of the creature that she
loved best upon earth, yet who was sufficiently
conscious of her shortcomings as to make her
doubt the wisdom of her own decision. . . .
Painful and confused are these gropings after
wisdom in the minds of human beings, who
have not that firm reliance upon their own in-
fallibility of judgment, that carries stronger-
minded folks with untroubled consciences over
everything, even enabling them to ascribe the
disasters arising from their own mistakes, to
fate, providence, or some influence that it
was not possible for them to foresee or
evade.

"And what would you say, Miss Mignon,"
she said at last, "if I was to tell you that I'd
got a love-letter in my pocket at this very
particular moment?"

"Say!" cried Mignon in delight, "why,
that it was the luckiest thing in the world,
and that it would *more* than make up for the

wheel coming off the barrow ! And to think that you'd got it bottled up there all this time, and never said a single word about it ! Why, if anybody wrote *me* a love-letter, I shouldn't be able to sit down for a week, much less do plain sewing !"

" And supposing," said Prue, her hand in her pocket, " that somebody should take the trouble to write a love-letter, not to me, Miss Mignon, but to *you ?*"

" That is so likely, is it not," said the girl, laughing, " when I do not know a single man who is not fat and bald, and a long way past forty ? No, no, Prue, only *young* people write love-letters, and I do hope he is very deeply in love with you, because I don't want to read a cool love-letter, but a *hot* one !"

" He's just mad with love," said Prue, nodding, "but it's not with *me,* Miss Mignon, it's with *you !*"

" *Me ?*"

" You !"

" Somebody in love with ME ?"

" Somebody in love with *you !*"

" *Not* a schoolboy, or the sexton, or the postman, or the chimney-sweep ?" said Mignon, her eyes growing rounder and rounder as she looked at Prue.

" No, miss, a gentleman."

" Grown up ? out of jackets ?"

" La ! yes, miss, in tails.   Looks as if he'd been born in 'em."

" Prue," said Mignon in a tone of utter disbelief, " are you *joking ?*   Are you making all this up because I said I thought, if I tried it, I should *like* a beau ?"

" No, miss, it's gospel truth."

" What an *extraordinary* thing !" said Mignon, drawing a deep breath, " what an altogether *outrageous* thing—to fall in love with *me*, of all people in the world !   And where on earth did he do it, and what could have inspired him with the gigantic idea of— love ?"

" It was at Hampton Court, miss," said Prue, " and so far as I can make out, it's the very gentleman as you and Miss Lu-Lu nearly upset cutting round that tree in the avenue."

" I certainly made an impression upon *him*," said Mignon soberly, " and on his hat, and his shins, or I am very much mistaken ! Are you quite sure, Prue, that he is not *pretending,* just to pay me out for being so rude to him ?"

"No," said Prue, nodding impressively, "he's in earnest, there's no mistake about *that.*"

" And indeed," said Mignon, " I am beginning to think he *must* be, to do anything so desperate as to write me a *love-letter !* Why, Lu-Lu never had one in all her life, and she is seventeen years old, and we should *both* have been so much obliged to any one who would write us one, just to see what it would be like !"

Prue, looking down on her needlework, smiled. Miss Sorel's school was a well-ordered one, the supervision of letters strict, and many an ardent effusion had she seen transmitted to the flames, instead of to the girl to whom it was addressed. Contraband music too, breathing sentences quite as tender, and far better expressed than the accompanying *billets*, was invariably passed on to the music-master and learnt in perfect good faith by the pupils, who dreamed not that they were giving utterance to their lovers' fervent sighs, when they underwent the awful ordeal of their singing-lessons from that most terrible of professors, Herr Klingholz.

She could have told many a story too of treasure-trove, discovered in the course of her morning and evening weeding before service began, in the hymn and prayer books left in the church pew from Sunday to Sunday, and of the enormous discomposure of the gilded youth of Lilytown, who had hoped by this *ruse* to circumvent the stately mistress of Rosemary. But of all this, the girls, most of whom were very young, had suspected nothing, believing the horde of recurrent young gentlemen who waited upon their footsteps to be but one of the natural and inevitable adjuncts of a ladies' school, and at once a flattering but disappointing fact.

" If only," said Mignon, emerging from her trance of amazement, with a sigh of delight, "he had thought of it earlier, how it would have helped to pass the time, to be sure ! Why, it would have been *twice* as amusing as Grimm's Goblins, and a *thousand* times better than the wheelbarrow !"

" P'r'aps I'm wrong in telling you about it at all," said Prue, "but Lor ! he began to write to you long afore you thought of the barrow; you've only had that a week, but *he've* been writing love-letters to you for the last *two*."

" *What !*" cried Mignon, starting up ; "he took the trouble to write to me, and you never even told me ? Oh ! I will never, never forgive you," she cried, stamping her foot; "and when you knew how *dull* I was too !"

And here, with shame I confess it, the tears poured down her cheeks, for Mignon was a representative of that enormous class of women whose anger holds off exactly long enough to say all that they wish, and perhaps

bang a door or two, ere dissolving into in-
dignant, passionate weeping.

"*Good* Lord ! what a sweet little shrew !"
thought the wallflower to itself.

" La !" said Prue, retreating as far as she
could, "what a temper you've got, to be
sure, Miss Mignon ! I misdoubt me, but I've
done wrong in telling you of it, though if
'twasn't for a little circumstance as happened
no later than last night, p'r'aps you'd never
have knowed nothing of the matter at all."

" A circumstance !" cried Mignon, a flicker
of April sunshine coming and going in her
blue eyes ; "and pray what was that ?"

" Nothing much," said Prue. " Only when
I told him I couldn't and wouldn't bring you
no love-letters, since you was left in my charge
while Miss Sorel was away, he just took me
by the shoulders, and shook me with all his
might and main till the breath was all but
out of my body, and said he, ' I'll ask you to
take her no more letters, you fool, but I'll
just go straight to her myself.' When he'd
done, I said to myself, ' That's *real* love and

no mistake, and I don't know as it's my duty to stand between 'em.' "

"Did he really?" said Mignon, looking delighted; "he must be *very* fond of me to do that, Prue! It reminds me wonderfully of William the Conqueror and Matilda!"

Here she sat down on the parsley-bed, obeying the universal law of womankind, that impels it to start up at the merest suspicion of good or bad news, and sit down under the shock of the reality, whichever it may be.

"I don't know nothing about William and Matilda," said Prue, to whom history was a myth, while to-day was a matter of serious and profound consideration. "But his way of doing things made me think he loved you true, and meant honest by you, and there's no denying I should be glad and thankful to see you settled in a home of your own, for more reasons nor one, and so——"

"But I don't want your reasons," cried Mignon, "I want the letter," and seizing Prue's pocket, she turned it inside out, and

the last thing coming uppermost, proved to
be a big square envelope, decidedly the worse
for wear, indorsed in a bold legible handwriting :

> " MISS MIGNON,
>
>> *Rosemary,*
>>
>>> *Lilytown.*"

" There !" said Prue, surveying it, " I don't
know whether it's one of the old ones ; but I
daresay it'll be just as good to read if it is—
I guess he says pretty much the same in all
of 'em !"

" I don't think I'll read it to-day," said
Mignon, holding it a little way off, and looking at it admiringly. " It can't come *twice*
in one's lifetime to open one's first love-letter,
you know ! I'll save it up as a great treat
until to-morrow. What do people *generally*
say in love-letters, Prue ?"

" Rubbish !" said Prue, rolling up her
work. " One don't look for sense from
lovers, miss !"

CHAPTER IV.

" She hath one of my sonnets already : the clown bore it, the fool sent it, the lady hath it: sweet clown, sweeter fool, sweetest lady !"

MIGNON sat on a wooden chair set full in the sunlight, hemming a pocket - handkerchief, at nine o'clock in the morning. She wore a white dimity gown, tied in at the waist, throat, and wrists with ribbons that matched the colour of her eyes exactly, and altogether she and the young June morning became each other vastly, and seemed expressly made for one another—or so the wallflower thought, that was as nearly as possible facing her, though considerably out of the range of her ordinary regard. She was but an indifferent worker,

and took advantage of every possible pretext
to give her needle a rest—quarrelling with a
stray sunbeam that had fallen in love with her
eyelashes ; scolding a naughty lazy butterfly
who came fluttering past in the desultory, idle
fashion of his tribe ; making fun of an indus-
trious bee who had got into the garden by
mistake, and, finding cabbages instead of
flowers, went buzzing about in a fussy discon-
tented fashion.   She said good-morning to an
ancient snail who came slowly by, as though
he found existence rather a troublesome affair
than otherwise, and condoled with him concerning the law of nature that compelled him
to carry his house on his back, at the same
time pointing out that the scheme had its
advantages, since he need never be at all
afraid (like other folks) of his dwelling being
pillaged, or burnt down while he was abroad.
"And as for *you*, sir," she said to a Polly-
wash-dish who was whisking his long tail up
and down the gravel walk at a safe distance
from her, "if you had any shame in you at
all, you would *blush* for your own deficiencies

—are you aware that the linnet has *sixty-four* notes in his register, while you have not a single one worth mentioning? While as to washing up dishes, I don't believe you ever do anything half as useful, for it's my belief that you're a regular gadabout, disgraceful flirt, with a better opinion of yourself than anybody else has, your wife included—there! Still I think I would rather be a pert silly creature like you than sitting on a wooden chair hemming a handkerchief that has been in process of hemming three months, and may consider itself lucky if it's finished in thirty more!"

Here she pricked her finger, and instantly put it in her mouth, obeying a strictly feminine impulse that made the wallflower, which was a close observer of men and manners, smile.

" Now if *he* were here," she said, thinking aloud, as was her wont in the solitary old garden, " I suppose he would put himself into a dreadful state of mind, and of course I should say it was nothing at all, but look as if I were enduring *agonies;* and then he would go down on his knees (as the fairy princes always do) and entreat me to let him look at it—and then, should I let him, or should I not ? I don't know."

She took the pricked finger out of her mouth, and drew from her pocket a letter, at which she looked with immense complacency, holding it away from her with her head on one side, bringing it nearer to her by degrees, finally depositing it in her lap, and resuming the handkerchief with a deep sigh of satisfaction.

" It's the most extraordinary thing I ever heard in my life," she said, shaking her fair head. " It can't be my looks—Muriel is lovely, and I'm not a bit like her, no two sisters could be more unlike ; and it can't be my money, for I haven't a rap ; so it must be all downright, substantial *me* that Mr. Rideout's fallen in love with. Ah ! it's a finer thing to be loved for what you *are* than what you've *got*, because the looks and the money often run away from you, but *you* stop, unless you die, that is to say ; and of course when you're dead you don't think of whether people like you or not! After all it was a *mercy* I pelted round that tree, in all probability he never would have seen me if I had not, and then the chance would have gone by, and perhaps I should never have had a lover all the days of my life (it's not likely *two* people would be so mad as to fall in love with me), but now—I'm *somebody.* When I got up this morning I said to myself, 'Most likely Mr. Rideout's getting up too, and I shouldn't wonder if he's thinking about—*me.* He will go out and look for Prue by-and-by, to see if she has got a letter from—*me.* When he has read it, he will sit down (entirely and solely upon my account) to write to—*me ;* and then he will go out with it again, and his head quite full of—*me.*' Only to think of it—a little person that nobody owns, and nobody loves, to be of so much importance all in a minute to another person as *that !*

"'*Am I never to have a chance of speaking one word to you, Miss Mignon?*' he says. '*Shall I*

never find means to elude the vigilance of that
she-dragon, Mrs. Prue ?'

"Though, indeed, that is not kind of him,"
she said, looking down at the open letter, and
smiling ; "after he had shaken her into
bringing me the letter too !

" '*And if you will not hold your finger up*
to give me this same chance, I will force my
way to your side and tell you—what will I not
tell you, my lovely, childish little sweetheart ?'

" And he ends up :
         " '*Your faithful lover,*
             "' PHILIP RIDEOUT.'

" It is very short," she said, laying it down
and surveying it with regret, whereby it
would appear that Mr. Rideout thoroughly
understood the art of love-letter writing as
expounded by Mr. Weller, who advised a
lover to make his letter very short, but very
sweet. "For then," said he, "she vill vish
there vos more."

" If Prue does not come soon," said Mignon, " I shall be obliged to go down on my knees and tell Bumble all about it, and though of course he would not understand, still he would be better than *nothing!*"

She fell to hemming again out of sheer desperation, though certain smiles and stray dimples occasionally relieved the gravity of her countenance, and were duly noted by the wallflower that watched her as unwinkingly as though it had never in all its life had so curious a subject for study as a school-girl, of sixteen or thereabouts, in a white dimity gown. Prue appeared, bearing a work-box and a pile of calico.

" Oh, there you are at last!" cried Mignon, " but you may as well put that stuff away, for I'm not going to do any more needlework to-day. I'm going," she said gravely, " to do the most particular thing I ever did in all my life, and I want you to help me. Tell me, Prue, did you ever write a *love-letter?*"

" Once by whiles, miss. Why?"

" Never you mind.   What did you say ?"

" I can't recollect, miss, 'tis so long ago."

" But you can at least remember how you *began* it?" said Mignon anxiously ; " the very first you ever wrote—you can't have forgotten *that* ?"

" Yes, miss," said Prue gently, " I have forgotten even that."

But she had not : no woman ever does forget what she said in her first love-letter ; and at that moment Prue's eyes saw not the work she held in her hands, but a round wooden table set in a country-house kitchen, a sheet of gilt-edged pink paper, a knot of violets, and what was written upon the page I cannot tell, but am very sure that Prue could, word for word.

" You see," said Mignon, frowning and looking wise, " there is always a right and a wrong way of doing everything, even to writing a love-letter, and it would be such a dreadful thing to take the wrong one, would it not ?"

" Drefful," said Prue ; " but you're not

thinking of writing to Mr. Rideout this morning ?"

"And why not ?" said the girl. "Don't you know that it is the rudest thing possible not to send an answer to a letter that you have received ?"

"I don't fancy that rule applies to billy-doos, Miss Mignon," said Prue dubiously, "and writing's a very dangerous thing. It don't so much matter what you says, miss; words is easy forgot, unless they happen to be particularly true and *stick;* but what you write, why there it is, and there you are—there's no getting out of it no-how."

"But I don't mind if it does," said Mignon. "I'm not going to say anything I mind *anybody* seeing! I only want to tell him that I'm very much obliged to him for his letter, and that I *hope* he will write me another one soon (for really there is very little in this one, and wouldn't fill half a page of our—but that's a secret), and ask him what on earth made him take a fancy to me, and send him my best love—and—and I think that's all, Prue !"

" All !" said Prue, aghast, " and about enough too, I should think ! Miss Mignon, Miss Mignon, you're as ignorant of the practices of courtship as a heathen ! Young ladies don't write like that the first time they put pen to paper to a young man ; they hold back a bit, are modest, for it's a drefful mistake to be forrard with a man—there's such a deal of selfishness in 'em, that if there's any doubt of getting a thing they perticler want, they'll pursue it like mad till it's overtook ; but if you tumble into their arms like a ripe peach, they'll drop you as sure as fate, miss, sooner or later. La ! the difference there is when a man's sure of a girl, and when there's a considerable doubt about it, so nimble and civil and wideawake when he's on his promotion, so easy and lazy when he's got her safe and sound, and knows he can pop his finger down upon her at any time !"

" Yes," said Mignon absently, for she had

long ago lost the thread of Prue's argument,
" but really it was very unlucky that Mr.
Rideout did not put any beginning to his
letter, for of course I could have put just the
same to mine. I would not for the world be
behind him in politeness, or offend him—
perhaps he would never write to me again,
and that would be dreadful !"

Prue threw up her hands in despair.

" Now what," said Mignon, " would you
say to ' *My dear Mr. Rideout* ' ?"

" No 'my,' " said Prue. " ' Dear Mr.
Rideout.' "

" Keep that in your head while I get the
things ready !" said Mignon, picking up her
desk from the ground, and arranging it on
her knee.

" Now then." " Dear Mr. Rideout," she
wrote in good intelligible round hand. On
ordinary occasions she wrote a rather pretty
scrawl, but on an occasion of such magnitude
as this she instinctively fell back upon the
obedient, careful caligraphy of her earlier
years. " Now I should like," she said, " to

tell him that I am sorry I ran up against
him in that rude manner with Lu-Lu, or he
may think I'm in the *habit* of doing such
things. Don't you think it might be as
well just to mention it, and start *fair*,
Prue ?"

"P'r'aps so," said Prue, considering ;
" though I should say that, on the whole,
miss, it being such a very awkward little
circumstance, the less said about it the
better."

"*First of all*," wrote Mignon, "*I must
beg your pardon for nearly knocking you
down that day in Bushey Park—I never did
such a thing before in all my life, and I never
will again, if I can possibly help it! I am
very much obliged to you for the letter you
sent me by Prue, and hope you will write me
another one soon, as I am so dreadfully dull
here, though, if it would not be a great trouble
to you, would you mind making it a little
longer ?*"

"And I should like," said Mignon, pausing
in her labours, "to say something nice and

kind, and complimentary about his personal
appearance, for in his letter he called *me*—he
actually did—' lovely !' Of course he did not
mean it, still I don't wish him to have all the
civility on his side, so can you think, Prue,
of any safe, polite remark that one might
make to a person with blue eyes and black
hair, when one did *not* admire either the one
or the other in a man ?"

" No, miss, I can't.   'Tis a delicate matter,
and you might say the wrong thing ; you'd
best let it alone."

" Oh, very well," said Mignon, looking
disappointed, " but it does seem a regular
pity to miss such a good opportunity ! *And
if you would not mind telling me,*" she wrote,
" *I should like so much to know what made
you take a fancy to me. Nobody ever did
before, or is ever likely to again ! Was it
because you thought I had nobody to care
about me, and so you were sorry for
.me ?*"

"That'll never do, miss," said Prue hastily.
" It's a bad notion for a man to have, that he

can either take or leave you because there's nobody else as is fond of you."

"Never mind the notion," said Mignon, "is it not the *truth?* And now for the finish, I declare it's almost as bad as the beginning ! *He* says, ' Your faithful lover ;' now wouldn't you think ' Yours very gratefully ' would be the proper thing ?"

" ' Yours truly,' or nothing," said Prue in horror, " that's the usual—the only *respectable* way of ending a love-letter, miss."

" I don't see at all why I should be *such a long way* behind him !" said Mignon discontentedly ; " but as you've written some yourself of course you ought to know all about it. ' With love,' then, ' yours truly !' "

"No love !" said Prue ; " kind regards, miss !"

"Kind regards, then," said Mignon, sighing. " With kind regards, yours truly, Mignon Ferrers !"

But on her own account she put in as P.S. : " I wanted to send my love to you, but Prue, who helped me to write this letter, would not

hear of it; indeed, she has been so troublesome, that I have a very great mind to
write my next love-letter to you *all by
myself!*"

CHAPTER V.

"I am one, my liege,
Whom the vile blows and buffets of the world
Have so incensed that I am reckless what
I do to spite the world."

IT was nine o'clock in the evening, and the dusk was stealing on apace, veiling the trees and houses of Lilytown delicately and imperceptibly, as though it were loath to confess that the happy summer day was dying, and the shadowy, silent night creeping slowly into life.

There brooded over the place that strange loneliness which at nightfall ever seems to attend places that are neither town nor country, that, while missing the cheerful sights and sounds of the former, do not possess the careless freedom and security of the latter; and the roads, planted at intervals with trees, were so absolutely deserted that it might have been a city of the dead, instead of a suburb but a few miles away from the great Babylon, whose mighty heart throbbed and beat out yonder—the home of millions of toiling, sorrowing, suffering men and women, who jostled each other day by day and hour by hour in the giant city, yet knew each other not; the class that dies from over-feeding and the one that dies from over-hunger, velvets and tatters, gold and dirt—all these went to and fro yonder, but the echo of their voices and lives spread not so far out as lonely, quiet Lilytown.

Prue, her shopping over, and basket in hand, set out on her homeward walk in a leisurely fashion, taking now and again a long refreshing sniff of the pure, fresh air, as though she liked it. She had not gone very far when footsteps, rapid and decided, came following after hers.

" *Him !*" she said, giving a little jerk of her head backwards, and quickening her walk with that inborn contrariety that makes the comparison of a woman to a shadow one of the pithiest, truest things ever uttered.

" Ah ! he's a bold one," she soliloquised, " a reg'lar handful as ever *I* saw."

A tall grey shadow stepped from behind a tree she was passing, and intercepted her. He came so swiftly and silently, that she half shrieked aloud, but being strong-nerved, turned the hysterical cry into, " I beg your pardon, sir !" and passed on.

It gave her an odd sensation of doubt and fear when, glancing downwards, she saw him still by her side, keeping pace with her step for step, and treading so lightly that his footfall sounded strange and ghostly in the stillness.

" Mrs. Prue," said the grey shadow, " you will not give the letter you have in your pocket to Mr. Rideout, who is now following us."

Prue stopped as though she had been shot, and for once in her life her breath literally went.

" And pray," she cried at last, peering into his face through the gathering dusk, " who may you be, and what do you mean with your *Mrs. Prues* and *letters?*"

" A friend," said the man in grey, " who would act a friend's part ; but we must move on, we shall be overheard."

Involuntarily she recommenced walking, compelled thereto, though unconsciously, by the strength of will of the man who addressed her.

" Mrs. Prue," he said quietly, " you have a little mistress whom you adore. She is left under your sole charge, committed to your most careful and vigilant keeping, yet you have conveyed to her a letter written by a man whose real name you do not know, at whose antecedents you cannot possibly guess, and, misled by you, and betrayed by you into a clandestine correspondence, she has replied to that letter. Her answer lies in your

pocket at this very moment. In your own
mind you have thought the matter out thus :
Here is my young mistress without any
relations, with next to no friends, who may
at any moment, by the death of her benefactress, be thrown penniless upon the world,
and compelled to earn the very bread she
eats ; and here is a lover, young, rich, madly
in love, who is able to take her out of all this
doubt and uncertainty, and, by making her
his wife, secure to her a home, and a certainly
provided for future. So far, your reasoning
(setting aside the young lady's own inclina-
tion) is good, and there is but one drawback
to your plan."

"And that is ?" cried Prue, coming up,
gasping from the cold bath of amazement
into which his latter remarks, even more
than any of the previous ones, had plunged
her.

"That he is not at liberty to woo any
woman honestly. Judge then what you are
doing by promoting a correspondence between
your innocent young mistress and this man,

and remember that one encroachment paves
the way for another—the next will be, his
making his way into her presence."

"Good Lord!" said Prue half aloud; "now
I wonder who's to know which is the honest
man, and which is the rogue?"

"If I were a rogue," said the man by her
side, "I should scarcely be taking this trouble
to serve your mistress, should I?"

"Your voice sounds honest," she said at
last, "but I can't see your face, or I should
know in a minute if you're telling me the
truth. Anyway I'll promise you this, he
shan't have the letter till I've found out
whether or no it's lies you've been telling
me this night—there!"

Mr. Rideout, his patience thoroughly ex-
hausted, actuated moreover by some suspicions
that he was resolved if possible to verify, here
took half a dozen hasty steps forward, and
joined the waiting-woman and her companion.

"Good-evening, Mrs. Prue!" said he; "I
hope I don't intrude?"

Paul Pry's famous phrase fell from his lips

in so rollicking, dare-devil a fashion that
Prue, for all her fears, could not forbear
smiling as she replied :

" No intrusion, sir ; certainly not."

They were at the moment passing a gas-
lamp newly lit, that plainly revealed the two
men's faces to each other and to Prue, and
the eyes of the former met in a sudden keen
scrutiny, that hardened instantaneously—on
Rideout's part at least—from inquiry into
hostility. If such a thing were possible, I
should say that from this moment they
became enemies, with no one-sided enmity,
as when one man hates another virulently,
while the latter is too indifferent or peaceable
by nature to return the compliment with
vigour, but equally, with a thorough and
hearty reciprocity of feeling that would
enable them to fight each other well, if in
the battle of life they came to be pitted the
one against the other.

" So," said Rideout to himself, " sets the
wind in that quarter ? I must hasten opera-
tions a little, or he will be cutting in before

me, and heavily as I am handicapped by cursed ill-luck, no one but I shall win her —I swear it !"

Prue also had profited by the momentary opportunity afforded by the lamp, and in her own mind had drawn a comparison between the two men that was surely unjust, seeing that the colour of a man's hair, or the shape of his features, oftentimes affords no clue whatever to the qualities of heart, mind, and brain that he may possess.

Quickening her steps, for she felt about as comfortable as may he who is planted between two barrels of gunpowder that may explode at any moment, Prue suddenly discovered that the man in grey had disappeared from her side ; that even as he came, so had he departed, in impenetrable silence and mystery.

" Well, I'm sure !" ejaculated Prue, staring alternately at the sky, the earth, and the trees, as if she expected them to inform her which direction he had taken. " I wonder am I bewitched to-night, or *dreaming ?*"

" Dreaming," said Mr. Rideout curtly,

angry at what he believed to be her deceit-
fulness and double-dealing; "perhaps, however, you'll try and collect your wits
sufficiently to answer me a question or two.
In the first place, who was that man that
left you a moment ago?"

Left her! Had he then disappeared by
so prosaic a fashion as *leaving* her? To
Prue's excited imagination he was hovering
somewhere near in an atmosphere of brim-
stone, for who but the Evil One himself
could have told her the thoughts, plans, and
hopes that she had locked in her own breast,
nor ever breathed to any living creature?

"Do you hear me, woman?" cried Mr.
Rideout; "who was that man?"

"That, sir," said Prue with unexpected
spirit (why does the accusation of being a
woman ever carry to the female mind an
intolerable sense of unmerited insult?), "is
my affair."

"No!" he cried, quick as light, "I am
pretty sure that it is mine. Doubtless you
are a very good woman, but I'll be shot

if you're a handsome one, and that man is no lover of yours, but of—your mistress."

" He ?" cried Prue in amazement, and re-assured at the notion of the stranger being anything so commonplace as a lover. " Why, I never saw him in all my life until to-night !"

" And he did not ask you to convey to her any letter or message ?" persisted Rideout, who judged his neighbour by himself, and expected to find no virtues in him that he did not discover in himself.

" No indeed !" said Prue. " On the con-trary——"

She stopped abruptly.

" On the contrary,"—he repeated.

With some men thought is naturally slow, the result of antecedent fact or cautious reflection ; with others, instantaneous, and partaking of the character of intuition, and to the latter class belonged Rideout. More-over, guilt, that marvellous quickener of the intelligence, had greatly intensified his powers of observation, so that it was in the manner of an assertion, rather than a question, that he cried :

"So he knows something of me; he *warned* you against me, did he ?"

Utterly unable to discover the connecting link between her own hasty disclaimer and his apparently *mal-à-propos* remark, that yet, inconveniently enough, hit truth in the bull's-eye, Prue felt more than ever convinced that the devil was abroad to-night; and like the friar, surprised in the midst of a savoury meal on a fast-day by a terrific thunderstorm, who could not imagine why there should be such a fuss about a little bit of bacon, Prue felt it to be something altogether beyond her philosophy that the innocent love-letter lying in her pocket should be the occasion of so general an upheaval of all things.

" Can't you *speak ?*" he cried impatiently.

His imperious tone, albeit such as he habitually used with his servants, was one to which Prue was by no means accustomed, so that it was with a certain dignity that she replied :

"Them as has got nothing to fear has no call to trouble themselves about what folks says of them, sir; and I'm misdoubting me but I've done wrong in telling Miss Mignon, and I'll tell her no more—but, sir," her voice broke off suddenly, "how could you have the heart to try and deceive her so, and she so young, and lonely, and all?"

"Yes," he said, his voice altogether changing, "she is very young and very lonely. . . . A man would be hard-hearted indeed who sought to harm such as she . . . . and you think me as bad as that?" he cried, turning suddenly round upon Prue.

In his voice, as in that of the man who had but now spoken with her, was a ring of honesty, that she, being so purely honest herself, could not fail to recognise and acknowledge. For a moment she hesitated; then, making up her mind more quickly than she had ever done in her life before:

"Sir," she said, "if you love my young mistress as she ought to be loved, and if you're still wishful to get her for your wife (as you

told me the other night you was), then 'twill
be no such great matter to wait for her till
Miss Sorel comes back, when you'll be able
to court her as ladies is used to be courted,
not as if she was a poor serving-maid like
me."

"I have seen your Miss Sorel," he said,
"a cold, proud, handsome woman, who has
outlived the memory of her youth; who will
choose my little sweetheart's husband as she
would buy her an instructive book or a useful
gown; who will judge a man by his past
history, not by the capacities he may possess
for future good——"

He broke off, he had forgotten to whom
he was speaking, and that this woman could
not possibly understand him . . . how could
she, when his heart was to himself a dark
and bitter riddle that he had not yet solved?

"Sir—Mr. Rideout," said Prue firmly,
"if there's any reason why you shouldn't
come after Miss Mignon, if it's the leastest
wrong that you'll be doing her in trying to
win her love, then, sir, let me pray you to

go your ways and leave her in peace, for 'tis
a precious young life, and there's trouble
enough in store for her without any more
coming to her through a sweetheart—and
there's other beautiful young ladies in the
world besides her."

"There is only one Mignon . . . ." he said.
"Hark ye !" he cried impetuously, "any man
who tells you that I mean anything but
honestly by her, lies, for God knows I love
her too dearly to bring the shadow of sin or
shame upon her innocent head ; but there
are things that, told you by a stranger, might
make you believe me to be dishonourable and
unworthy of her, and such things I charge
you not to believe or repeat to her ; she could
never again be to me what she now is if one
doubt or fear of me had ever dimmed the
crystal purity of her mind. . . ."

"And if it's the truth you're telling me, sir,"
said Prue, touched in spite of herself, "and
if you love her so well as that, and are free
to court her honest, then I'll tell her no
word agen you ; but more than this I cannot

promise, nor will I take any more letters from you to her, nor from her to you."

"From her to me?" he repeated rapidly. "Have you then given her a letter from me —has she replied to it?"

Prue, making no reply, quickened her pace. On one point her mind was made up—she would keep her word to the stranger, whoever he might be, and the letter should be given back that night into the hands of her mistress. For the rest, Rosemary was but a few steps away, and it was with a sigh of relief that she pushed open the gate, and passed into the carriage-drive that approached the house in a circular form, having in its centre, and opposite the hall-door, a colony of thriving evergreens and shrubs. Was it fancy, or did she see, some distance ahead of her, a gleam of something white or grey? She could not be sure.

"Not so fast," cried Rideout, dashing after her; "you've not answered my question yet."

A dozen steps more would bring her to the

hall-door, and she would be safe, or so she thought, having reckoned without her host, for he caught her by the arm, holding her so tightly that to move was impossible.

"*Now*," he said, "did your mistress reply to that letter, or did she not?"

The light from the hall lamp fell upon Prue's ugly, perturbed countenance, and on the dark, reckless beauty of his.

"You are deceiving me," he cried angrily, "I see it in your face. *What's that?*" For Prue's hand had involuntarily tightened upon the pocket containing the letter, and his keen glance had instantly detected the gesture. "Ha!" he cried, "upon my soul I believe you are hiding something there." With a dexterous movement of his sinewy hand, he wrenched hers away, snatched the letter from the pocket, glanced at the address, and then tossed hand and letter high above his head in triumph. "You fool!" he cried scornfully, "so you meant to *cheat* me out of it—you thought yourself a match for Philip Rideout, did you?" Then his manner and voice changed all in a moment: " A love-letter from Mignon . . . . my little Mignon . . . ." he said . . . .

A hand and grey-coated arm issued noiselessly from the laurel-bush behind him, a finger and thumb alighted like a butterfly on the lightly-held letter, closed on it, and vanished as noiselessly as they had appeared.

CHAPTER VI.

"A falsehood in its contrary, as great
As my trust was."

THE birds were chattering, twitter-
ing, gossiping, flirting, and quarrelling as energetically as though
they had not had the use of their tongues
for six months, instead of six hours—for a
bird's summer night is a very little longer.

A young man in waistcoat and shirt-sleeves,
who stood on a ladder, and leaned his arms
on the top of the garden-wall, turned round
once or twice impatiently, as though he would
have liked to scatter the gossipers, but they
took no notice of him—not they!

Man may have dominion over the beasts of

the field, but it is to be doubted if he have any over the birds of the air, save that which brute force commands.   He may capture, torture, and destroy their bodies, but their spirits he reaches—never.

The dog clings with a more than human fidelity to the hand that chastises and caresses him, the cat creeps homeward night by night to the home that feeds and shelters her, all creation bows more or less to the yoke imposed upon it—all save the birds, who ask of man no other boon than that of liberty—liberty to abandon themselves (nobly regardless of the morrow) to their own glorious element, to live or die in it, as Heaven wills.

They care no more for his frowns than his smiles ; his angry passions affect them no more than does his tender pity for them when they are starved, and cold, and wretched . . . . a flirt of the wings as long as they will fly, a scrap of a song as long as their slender throats can utter sound, and away they go, heedless, irresponsive, thankless, neither to be tamed nor taught of man, unless he confines them in a cage, and deprives them of the final cause of their existence.

But mark! when he opens the door of the prison-house, how the bird will fly upward, like an arrow sped from a bow; weak and half dead though he may be, he prefers to die out in God's air, to dying in the care of man, who has not, with all his gentleness, contrived to establish his power over the brave self-reliant spirit, that breathes in that insignificant, frail little ball of feathers.

" I have a great mind to go over," said the person in shirt-sleeves; " for who is likely to be out at this time of the morning?"

He sat down on the wall, drew the ladder up after him, and dropped it on the other side.

" A means of exit if I am caught," he said to himself as he descended, " but that's not likely. A dull place," he added as he stood on the gravel-walk that ran round the goose-berry, currant, and raspberry bushes that in due season provide Miss Sorel's table with fruit-pies, and looked about him. And in truth it had not much to recommend it, now that the early freshness of spring had departed, and the goodly ripeness and riches of late summer had not yet crowned it with their plenty.

Opposite him was set Mignon's wooden chair, and on the ground by its side reposed a bulky volume of Grimm's "Goblins." Opening it he saw written on the title-page, " Mignon, her book," and he smiled as he laid it down again.

Under the chair lay the half-finished handkerchief, and beside it a tiny silver thimble; the latter he tried to fit on the tips of each of his fingers in turn—unsuccessfully. Turning round to give the garden a last stare preparatory to remounting the ladder, he found himself face to face with a young woman. Now, at six o'clock in the morning, young women are as a rule to be found in their beds, so that the trespasser had some excuse for looking, as he felt, profoundly astonished, and very much taken aback.

He might also have looked a fool had not

his features been turned by Nature rather in the direction of wisdom than folly—an inestimable boon to him who receives it, since the man who looks wise and does foolish things, is ever reckoned more sensible than he who looks a fool but acts like a man of wit, the countenance being open to all eyes, while his motives and actions are not.

Mignon (I can't tell why or wherefore she did it, but she did) blushed, and it being the first time she had ever blushed at the sight of a man, she overdid the colour very much, or the colour overdid her, until she looked like a rose that glowed freshly with every breath that stirred its heart.

She faced him thus, full front, for a quarter of a minute, after which she looked at him as calmly as though she wore the ordinary complexion of a maid at six o'clock in the morning, and said :

" And pray *who are you ?*"

There was a moment's silence, then the answer came,

" I am Adam, the gardener."

He made a slight gesture towards the ladder and garden beyond.

"O!" she said, and by now her face was swept as clean of colour as though the red rose had turned to a white one. Perhaps she had blushed because she thought him to be Rideout; perhaps she was disappointed—who can tell?

"And if you are the gardener from next door," she said, frowning, "pray what do you do in *here*? If the fruit were ripe I should have my suspicions about you, for we lost twelve peaches and nine nectarines last year, but really, just now," she lifted her head and glanced about her disdainfully, "we have nothing here but—snails!"

If it be the property and sign of virtue to indignantly repudiate unjust suspicion, then was not Adam virtuous; for he let the slur on his probity go by, and merely remarked:

"They're very bad this year, miss—snails."

"And it is not at all polite to walk into other people's gardens in this way," said Mignon, sitting down and picking up her work and thimble. "I'm sure I don't know what Miss Sorel would say if she could see you— you must never do it again, you know!"

"Of course not, miss," said Adam, backing towards the ladder; "not but what I should be very happy to be of use to you at any time: and if you should happen to want any little odd jobs done about the place, such as weeding, miss, or the plants watered, or anything of that sort, you've only got just to pop your head over the garden-wall, and say *Adam*, and I'll be with you in a moment."

"Thank you—Adam," said Mignon doubtfully. "The fact is, I *should* be glad of a little assistance sometimes, especially when I let the fowls out. Bumble always tries to fly away, and it would be such a dreadful thing for all his wives if he did—still I don't think I can call you—your master may not like it, to say nothing of our having no ladder; it's so very *mannish*, you see, for a ladies' school —so I don't quite see how I can pop my head over the wall—thank you all the same!"

"Why as to the ladder, miss," said Adam,

" that's easily managed, for I can leave you this one; and as to my master, he won't make any objections—he's away."

" Don't talk in that manner," said Mignon, frowning again; " it's immoral. You ought to do exactly the same behind his back as you do to his face."

Adam coughed. There was nothing remarkable in the cough, but somehow it set Mignon asking herself whether she would have liked for Miss Sorel to see the love-letter she had received, and the one she had written, the day before.

She looked the gardener full in the face for the first time, and met his eyes. Honest eyes they were, of that grey colour that is usually supposed to denote great intellectual power, but small capacity for loving; whereas it is rather the true lover's colour, being less changeable than the blue, and more expressive than the brown or black; clear and reasonable when the passions are at rest, darkening and flaming into splendid earnest when the heart is awake and astir.

"What a strange face for a gardener," thought Mignon, her eyes travelling slowly downwards, and resting on his earth-stained hands.

"Has your master a pretty garden—over there?" she said.

"Yes," he replied, "and plenty of flowers all a-blow; and a fountain and summer-house and shady walks—it's a gay place, very."

He stood before her looking down upon the slim young figure, the slowly-moving needle, the curly bent head; his whole energies, and they were not few, concentrated upon the feat of inventing some excuse whereby he might be licensed to remain looking at her a few moments longer.

"It is a fine morning," he said; but whether this remark was the result of the cudgelling of his brains, or a determined attempt to compel a glance of surprise from her at its egregious absurdity, it would be hard to say.

She looked up, wondering why he did not go away . . . she had, in fact forgotten his presence, for her thoughts were fixed upon more serious matters—or so, at least, she considered them to be.

" It could not well be finer," she said.

There was a little pause, while the girl glanced at the young man as men and women generally have a way of doing at a different class of people to themselves, less as though they are creatures of flesh and blood like themselves, than as at inanimate goods and chattels created for their especial convenience.

" It is not going to rain," said Adam, either from sheer stupidity, or with some latent hope that his witless folly might win from her a smile at his own expense.

But, alas ! not only did she not smile, but, appearing to consider that this remark required no answer at all, worked industriously on.

" Good-morning, miss !" he said at last; " and now," thought he, " she will have to look me in the face again."

" O, good-morning," she said, without

raising her eyes. " I thought you were gone long ago !"

He mounted a few rungs of the ladder, lingered, looked back, lost himself for a full minute in the contemplation of that dainty rose-leaf face, then said, in the most modest of voices, " Good-*morning*, miss !"

" Good-morning !" she said abstractedly, and without looking up.

What was her surprise to hear at least two minutes later a voice remarking, high above her, " *Good*-morning, miss !"

It was too much. The smile for which he had waited flashed out like a ray of sunlight upon the petals of a flower, and all her dimples —he had never had a really good view of them before—showed bravely as she looked up and said for the third time, " Good-morning !" But even on the top of the wall he paused to gaze down upon her ere he dropped on the other side, and vanished.

" What an extraordinary person !" said Mignon aloud. " But oh, I am so dreadfully hungry !"

As though in answer to the wish, Prue at this moment appeared, her eyes fixed upon the tray she carried, and that contained the girl's breakfast, which consisted of a cup of coffee, a plate of bread-and-butter, and a brown egg of not more than two days old, if its outward appearance did not sadly belie its inner.

" There !" said Prue, setting down the tray on Mignon's lap. " I got it for you as quick as I could, but what made you come out so early this morning ?"

" The birds made such a noise," said Mignon, tasting her coffee, " and, as I couldn't sleep, I got up. Now what do you suppose has happened to me this morning ? What would you say if I told you I had already had a *visitor* ?"

Prue jumped ; it was more than a start— it was a jump.

" A visitor, miss !" she said, turning pale, " and pray who might that be ?"

" A young man," said Mignon, tapping the brown egg smartly, " and an uncommonly good-looking one too! I am going to begin a diary to-day, and write in it, 'Spoke to a *young* man for the first time in my life, and *he* was'——"

"Who?" cried Prue breathlessly.

"Ah!" said Mignon gaily. "Wouldn't you like to know? He alighted from the clouds, or, more vulgarly speaking, arrived by the aid of a ladder; and he came after, at least I should think he must have, as there was nothing else here but me—what do you *think?*"

"I don't know, Miss Mignon," said Prue, breathless with impatience; "what a teaze you are to be sure!"

"*Snails!*" said Mignon, looking regretfully at the now empty egg-shell, and turning it upside down, whereby it was metamorphosed from a respectable wreck to a despicable sham. "And whenever I want to speak to him I'm to pop my head over the garden-wall and call out——"

"Yes," said Prue, on tenter-hooks, "call out *what?*"

" *Not* Mr. Rideout!" said Mignon. "Though, indeed, it is almost a pity. Just think of the opportunities one would have for writing and receiving love-letters over a wall with a PAIR of ladders !"

" Then, if 'twasn't Mr. Rideout," said Prue, considerably relieved, her suspicion reverting to the mysterious man in grey, " who could it have been, and what was his name, miss ?"

" It was only the gardener from next door, by name Adam," said Mignon. " And, do you know, I do not think that he is quite right in his head, for he wished me good-morning *three* times ! But tell me, do you think I shall get a letter from Mr. Rideout this morning ? It is very odd that he should not have sent one back to me when you gave him mine. Did he not seem *pleased* with it, Prue ?"

" Pleased enough," said Prue, turning away her head and recalling her last view of Rideout, dashing in mad pursuit of the thief who stole the letter.

" But didn't he *say* anything ?" said Mignon, puzzled by something in Prue's manner.

"Miss Mignon," said the woman slowly, " you'd best put him out of your head for a bit, anyways till Miss Sorel comes back, for p'r'aps it won't come to nothing after all ; and if it should turn out as he's no good——"

" No good !" said Mignon, " and ' nothing come of it !' why, you don't suppose I want to *marry* him—do you, Prue ? He can hold a pen, can he not, and has got a heart that *feels?* I don't want any more than that— indeed, I shouldn't know what to do with any other attentions ; and if he'll only go on writing me some nice love-letters, he may *be* as nasty as he pleases ! I'm not likely ever to speak to him, you know !"

" He's got a nerve of his own," said Prue, shaking her head, " a very wonderful nerve ; and it would not astonish me if he came swaggering into the garden this very minute and said, ' Miss Mignon, I've come to marry you ;' and it's my belief that if he said so you'd have to *do it*, miss !"

CHAPTER VII.

"T'S no matter what you *do*
If your heart be only *true*,
And his heart *was* true to Poll,"

said Mignon with great decision, as she liber-
ally dispensed the barley she held up in her
apron.

"I do wish," she went on, discarding
elegant quotation for commonplace prose,
and addressing the hens who scrambled and
fought, and pushed about her feet, "that you
would take pattern by Bumble, who is the
soul of politeness, instead of gobbling away
as though you were eating for a wager.
There can't be a ghost of a digestion among
you—perhaps that's why you're so tough and
nasty when you're eaten, whereas a little common politeness would make you far more

respectable in life, and satisfactory in death, if
only you could be brought to think so!
There!" she added, letting fall her apron with
its few remaining grains, and smiling at the
scrimmage they occasioned, "that's all; so
you need not perk your heads about in that
inquisitive way, for you won't get any more
for ever so long!"

She sauntered towards her accustomed
seat, and the feathered flock followed close
upon her heels, imagining that where so much
barley had been, more might yet be found.

"I can't help feeling sorry for you," she
said, sitting down and addressing them in-
differently; "you must find it so horribly
dull with nothing to do but scratch, scratch,
from morning till night, and look forward to
meal-times! You have not even the excitement of a good rousing quarrel now and then,
but peck at one another in a cowardly half-
hearted fashion, that can't relieve your feel-
ings one bit!"

The hens did not understand these remarks, and after standing about for some time

in various attitudes of despondency and expectation, they separated and spread about
the garden, all save Bumble, the cock, who
flew in a clumsy manner to the top of the
garden-wall, and from thence uttered a loud
and derisive cock-a-doodle-doo ! that awoke
warlike echoes in the gardens round about.

" Oh, Bumble !" cried Mignon in despair,
" that is the *third* time you have played me
this trick in one week ! Now I should like
to know how *on earth* I am to get you down
again ?"

But Bumble had no intention of leaving a
place that was evidently so much to his liking ;
so his only reply to this appeal was to flap his
wings fiercely, toss his head proudly, and
nearly dislocate his neck in a still louder note
of triumph than before, that was speedily
answered by his feathered brethren from
half a dozen adjoining gardens in every
imaginable key—high and clear, husky and
deep, shrill and quavering, hoarse and grum-
bling, weak and piping, every note in the
gamut of cock-a-doodle-doo-dum appeared to

have its representative, to swell the in-harmonious concert.

Having scaled the wall with a purpose, Bumble did not, however, pause to indulge himself in half an hour or so of crowing, as was his wont of mornings, when time hung particularly heavy on his hands, so set out with a lordly strut, and an evident intention of taking one of those unauthorised and vagabond rambles that were a source of peril to his neck, and grief to his mistress; for if he was brave, he was also foolhardy, and oftener than not returned from these excursions so severely mauled and beaten as to lead her to suppose that he had met with more kicks than halfpence by the way.

On one occasion, indeed, he remained away so long that a scarlet-combed and proudly-spurred gentleman of the neighbourhood appeared upon the scene, and was accepted by Bumble's lately obedient wives with that placidity which (added to greediness) appears to be the sole characteristic of the hen tribe. But, alas! one fine morning Bumble unexpectedly returned, and, discovering the profligate usurper of his affections, there ensued a great and grievous battle that was ever remembered by Mignon with fear and trembling, and that ended not until the doughty and justly enraged Bumble had, with great loss of blood and feathers to the enemy, achieved a signal victory over the daring intruder.

" He is going," she cried, her eyes anxiously fixed on the extreme tip of his vanishing tail. " Oh ! what *shall* I do ?"

Her eyes fell upon the ladder, and it put an idea into her head. To climb it was the work of a moment, and, on looking over the top of the wall, she discovered Adam working with his back turned to her.

" Adam !" she said breathlessly ; " quick— *Bumble!* he will be lost ! Don't you think you could manage to catch him for me ?"

But before Adam could answer, Providence interposed on Mignon's behalf in a somewhat ludicrous manner.

As Bumble went on his way rejoicing, his

toes well turned out, and perking his head from side to side, as though he were determined to see all that was to be seen on both sides of the way, he came suddenly face to face with a cat, who was also taking the air from an eminence, and whose approach he did not perceive till his feathers actually touched her fur.

He recoiled with so violent a start, that it would be folly to assert that a fowl has no nerves; indeed, he could not have looked more horrified if he had met a fox prepared to strangle and eat him, feathers, bones and all.

"What a godsend!" cried Mignon, in prodigious excitement. "If only she would chase him back!"

"If only they would stay looking at each other for ever," thought Adam, gazing up at the innocent, childish face that bloomed in all its delicate colours high above him.

But, alas for his hopes, the matter was decided in a few seconds. Puss claiming the right of way, and Bumble being in far too much of a fluster to efface himself in her favour, she flew at him tooth and claw ; while he, reversing himself with extraordinary rapidity, raced homewards with outstretched neck and flapping wings, nor rested until he had floundered headlong into the bosom of the family he had so lately quitted.

" Oh !" said Mignon, fetching a deep sigh of relief, " that *was* lucky ! Good afternoon ! I'm just as much obliged to you as if you *had* caught Bumble, you know !"

She nodded blithely, and vanished so suddenly as to plunge Adam, who had by no means reckoned on so speedy a disappearance, into utter despair.

Were his wits never to be at hand when he wanted them ? he asked himself angrily, as he stood looking at the bare wall, that a moment ago had appeared to him the finest spectacle that earth could afford.

A good general, however, does not pause to bemoan a · blunder, he sets to work to instantly repair it, if possible. Not more than ten seconds therefore had elapsed ere he had mounted his ladder, and was looking over into the adjacent garden. Alas! it was empty of all save Bumble, who stood, the image of discomfiture among his wives, who may, for aught we know to the contrary, have been twitting him with the ignominious end of his expedition. "Such an opportunity," he said to himself ruefully, "and to have missed it like that!"

Apparently minded to take a little holiday, he folded his arms on the top of the wall, rested his chin upon them, and refreshed his eyes with a good stare at the prospect before him.

He did not appear to grow tired of this amusement until a certain faint sound in the distance struck upon his ear, whereupon, and with such extreme rapidity as might lead any one on the other side to suppose that the perch on which he stood had ingloriously collapsed, he disappeared from the summit of the wall.

Footsteps were coming into the garden, voices were drawing near, and in a very few moments he enjoyed the happiness of parting the wallflower's leaves, and getting an excellent bird's-eye view of Mignon and Prue.

The woman was, as usual, sitting down; the girl standing with her hands behind her back, and voice a little raised in positive assertion.

" Yes !" she was saying, " on one point I am resolved—we will *do something,* Prue ! we will lead a gay life, you and I, for at least three whole days, beginning at eight o'clock to-morrow morning ! And in the first place we will go to Madame Tussaud's."

" Yes, miss," said Prue, immensely relieved at finding Mignon's iniquitous proceedings resolve themselves into nothing worse than a visit to the wax figures.

" The day after to-morrow," continued Mignon, " we will go to Hampton Court— but not by train, or in any way that we have ever been before, or are likely to go again— we will go on *donkeys.*"

" No, miss, we won't," said Prue with unlooked-for decision; " you'll not demean yourself in that way while I've got the charge of you. But if we could hear of a respectable shay now——"

Prue was one of those persons who call anything that goes upon wheels a " chaise ;" and indeed it is a comfortable, well-sounding word that casts a halo of respectability about the most broken-down of conveyances, for, however bad may be the conveyance that Providence has thought fit to send you, you have but to reflect that in the days of old the finest conveyance was oftener than not dubbed a " chaise," to retain your dignity, and feel that after all things might be worse.

" A shay costs money," said Mignon, shaking her head, and pursing up her lips ; " you must have a man to drive, and then the horse will want a feed—and I have only got ten shillings and sixpence in the world to last me till Miss Sorel comes back. I must not spend all my money on trips, though, because—are all gardeners *handsome,* Prue ?"

The apparently irrelevant question bore

reference to something that was then in her mind.

" I don't know, miss—about the same as other folks, I s'pose. They're mostly dirty fellows—'bliged to be with the work they do—and terrible fond of their beer and 'baccy."

" But this one is not dirty at all," said Mignon, puzzled. " His shirt-sleeves are as white as snow ; and he does not look as if he were fond of beer—not in the least !"

" This one ?" said Prue, " and pray who may that be, miss ?"

" The gardener from next door," said the girl. " I saw him just now. He was going to help me to catch Bumble. Now do you think he would be very much offended if I were to offer him half a crown ? Then he would be sure to help me at any future time, and even keep an eye upon the fowls when I happen to be away."

" Offended !" said Prue, " he'd jump at it, miss. But why should you do that—when you've got so little, too ? And he won't be a bit grateful to you for it, neither ;" by which it would appear that Prue knew her own class thoroughly.

" But I don't want him to be grateful," said Mignon ; " it's enough pleasure to me, to *give* it. It's a great luxury," she added, sighing, " the greatest of all under the sun, to give !"

He must have been very greedy, as well as dishonourable, the young man who listened to the foregoing conversation, for at the young lady's first intimation of her intentions, he gave vent to a quickly stifled exclamation of delight !

" Half a crown," he said to himself. " I wonder when will she give it me ? To-morrow ? The day after, the next ? If I watched Prue safely off the premises and went over, might she not even give it me to-day ?"

He vowed in his heart that by hook or crook he would at the earliest opportunity make his way into her presence ; and, in case she should have forgotten her intention, LOOK

7—2

half-crowns at her with all his might—only
he must be quick about it, or she would spend
all her money; she might not have another half-
crown to give away for months and months,
and then where would *he* be ?

Clearly there was no time to be wasted ;
he must waylay her on the morrow (and here
a question as to the possibility of getting
suitable holiday attire in which to go to
Madame Tussaud's obtruded itself disagree-
ably upon his mind), and it should go hard
with him if he did not catch her away
from Prue, and gain the promised *pour-
boire.*

For the rest, no lover ever hung on the
varying expression of a capricious mistress's
eye more fondly and faithfully, than would he
on the tip of Bumble's vagabond tail. Troy
was taken by a stratagem. Rome was saved
by the cackling of geese ; why should not
Bumble be the means of guiding him to the
end to which his ambitions pointed ?

And he fell asleep that night as happy as
a king, with the vision before him of Mignon

presenting him with a bright, brand-new half-crown, while the pleasures of Hope were represented by the sight of Bumble majestically vanishing in the distance.

CHAPTER VIII.

"Ye who have yearned
    With too much love, will here stay and pity
    For the mere sake of truth."

IGNON stood with her hands behind her back, winking at Mr. Cobbett, who sat at the foot of the Sleeping Beauty, neatly dressed, with his snuff-box in his hand, and turning his head slowly from side to side, as though he were trying to overhear some of the pure English that he loved. She never could divest herself of the belief that he was as much alive as she herself was, and it would not have astonished her in the least if one day he had closed one of his wicked little eyes in a deliberate return wink at her, but he never did, and she presently turned away, saying to herself that really he was a gentleman of very little *esprit* after all.

She had long got over the amazed wonder with which she had at first beheld these gorgeously-attired ladies and gentlemen, and now liked them according to their histories, having her favourites, of course, and never failing to go and say, " How do you do ?" to the Princess of Wales, and Maximilian, Oliver Cromwell, Voltaire, and Liston as Paul Pry. To these she had already paid her *devoirs*, and now sat down before Henry and his six wives, thinking for the fiftieth time how exactly like a big fat, tyrannical turkey-cock he looked, surrounded by a flock of timid, helpless hens, all waiting to have their heads cut off. Surely he must have been made of strange stuff, that burly, clear-faced king, with those amorous blue eyes that spoke the language of love well, or his portraits sorely belie him, to keep his complexion as purely red and white as that of a village beauty in her teens, when he had so

many crimes lying upon his mind ? Did these
poor murdered queens come stepping softly to
his side when he lay a-dying, whispering, "How
does it taste to *you*, this bitterness of death ?"
He was but a sorry knave after all, in spite of
his kingly air and presence !

The morning was not very old yet, still a
few people were strolling about, and, as usual,
were to be seen half a dozen of those courting
couples who would not consider they had seen
London unless they paid a visit to the " wax
figures," and who combined the triple enjoyment of criticism, courtship, and refresh-
ment in a manner apparently highly agreeable
and satisfactory.

Perhaps because Mignon was so used to
them all, she found the waxen people a little
dull that morning, and fell to wishing that they
would open their impossibly pink lips and talk
to her, for everybody knows it is very one-sided
work to talk to people who never answer you.
Therefore it was with a decided sense of
pleasure that Mignon saw passing, at some
little distance from her, a somebody whose

back seemed familiar, yet unfamiliar to her eyes, a somebody who had a semi-bump-kinish air, as though his clothes and he were not on good terms with each other, and only when he was on the point of disappearing did she recognise the gardener, Adam.

She jumped up, and ran after him.

" Is that you, Adam ?" she said, delighted at having a chance of speaking to somebody ; " and have you got a little holiday to-day ?"

" Yes, miss," he said ; and the girl thought to herself a little enviously, how happy he looked, and how thoroughly he seemed to be enjoying himself !

" You could not possibly come to a better place to spend it," she said gravely ; and a sweet little mentor she looked, for all the world like a freshly-plucked bunch of violets, he thought, in her white gown and hat, with their dark-blue ribbons. " It will give you an excellent idea of English history, and every young man who wishes to improve his mind should know something of the great men of his country."

"Yes, miss," said Adam, with unabated gravity.

"Though I don't suppose you've got as far as *French* history yet," she said, apparently delighted with the sound of her own voice; "still, I dare say you may have heard of Marie Antoinette? *There* she is!" said the girl, nodding towards her. "Prue always calls her *Maria*, because she can't pronounce her name the right way."

"Ah!" said Adam; "some of those French words are quite beyond most folks."

"Of course they are," said Mignon with dignity, "and I should never advise you to *attempt* to understand them. The three ' R's ' are quite enough for any respectable young man, and ' a little knowledge is a dangerous thing.' "

"Yes, miss," he said, and waited for more.

Instructing him by the way, she came presently to a stop before Mary Queen of Scots.

"I think you must have heard of *her*," she said gravely; "everybody has. She was wicked, you know " (she shook her head and looked solemn); " she had too many husbands: just as Henry over there had too many wives; and they both got into a very bad way of killing off the ones they did not like, so that of course it was not *possible* for any one to approve of either of them."

" Of course not," said Adam, looking profoundly impressed, and only hoping that she might have time to expound to him the whole catalogue before Prue swooped down upon, and routed him.

But Mignon's thoughts had taken a new turn. She was looking towards the turnstile in the distance, through which people passed in twos and threes, all looking expectant and eager, some frightened.

" Adam," she said, " have you ever been into the Chamber of Horrors ?"

" Yes, miss, once."

" Was it *very* awful? Did it haunt you for days and weeks and months afterwards ?"

" No," he said, smiling a little ; " but were you thinking of going in ?"

" Should you say that a person would be likely to tumble down in a fit ?" she went on, disregarding his question.

" Not unless she were subject to fits at any other time."

" You see, it would be so awkward if there were nobody to pick one up !"

" You need not be afraid, miss !"

" Prue is no good, she would as likely as not tumble down too," she went on, apparently thinking aloud. " You are sure you would not like to go in again, Adam ?" looking at him much as a robin may at a respectable crow against whom he is plotting some fairy mischief.

" I should *love* to, miss."

" Then so you *shall*," she said briskly ; " but you mustn't speak to me, unless you see I'm *very* much frightened, only if you can't understand everything, and come to me, I'll explain it to you."

" Yes, miss."

" By the bye," she said, growing rather red and putting her hand in her pocket, " you smoke tobacco, Adam, do you not, and you drink *beer* ?"

" Yes, miss."

" Then will you—will you mind accepting a little *wherewithal* to buy some ?"

And with the true shamefacedness of the generous giver, she thrust the half-crown into Adam's hand, that did not close modestly and secretly upon the gift, as surely it should have done ; but, on the contrary, received it publicly, openly, the silver coin lying upon his open palm as a respectable fact that all the world was welcome to behold.

Adam looked musingly down at the half-crown, as though it were the first piece of money he had ever seen in his life.

" Thank you, miss," he said at last, and still looking at it, laid it away in his pocket.

Mignon heaved a sigh of relief ; thank goodness *that* business was over. Then she paid two sixpences at the turnstile, and, with a fast-beating heart, stepped over the threshold of the famous chamber,

that grisly abode of which she had heard
such terrible stories, but fetched a sigh of
relief when, on looking around, she beheld
no more or less than (at the first glance) a
waxen assemblage of ordinary men and
women, and circulating among them a score or
so of real flesh and blood people, who chat-
tered, stared, and gossiped, apparently quite
unimpressed by the atmosphere of murder
that they breathed.

And yet, when Mignon's eye was caught
by the cast of Ravaillac's head, taken after
death, and she went near to examine it—
when she noted the cruel, and slightly pro-
truded lips, the stealthy lurid eyes, the brand
of murderer that nature had imprinted upon
every line of his face, and that outlived the
inconceivable horror of the death he died—she
began to understand why this room was
indeed terrible, why it had so powerfully
affected the minds of some who entered it,
because it was a record of things true, things
accomplished, because every silent figure here
present was the representative of a cowardly

atrocious crime that had been committed—
because, side by side with the destroyer of
life, one beheld in imagination the victim or
victims, and saw enacted before one the
whole frightful tragedy. Would so many
tears have fallen when Mr. Irving walked
to his doom as Charles the First, had
the story been an imaginary one, had the
woes he represented been fictitious? The
lookers-on knew that it had all *happened*—
that in some such fashion as this the king
had bade his wife and little ones a long farewell; that in just such fashion he had walked
forth in the grey of the early morning, guiltless, to his doom.

Mignon had not been in the room sixty
seconds, when a gentleman, who had just
entered, and having by his side a young lady
caught sight of the girl's profile, and starting
violently, made a sudden step or two forward
as though to join her. Recovering himself
as quickly, however, he said something in a
low tone to his companion.

"Yes—let us go," she said coldly and

wearily; and what a strange voice it was, to issue from such young and beautiful lips !

" It was a foolish fancy—no more—that made me enter "—her tone changed with the last few words to a passionate wistfulness that belied their lightness, and words and tone alike, though uttered at some distance, pierced to Mignon's ears, and produced upon her an instantaneous and extraordinary effect. For some seconds she stood perfectly motion-less, absolutely incapable of either speech or movement; then, shaking off with a desperate effort the spell that bound her, she gazed wildly around.

" Muriel !" she cried.   " Muriel !"

And the cry sounded eerie and strange in the dismal room, and the people fell back from her as she ran hither and thither, with outstretched arms and a breathless look of joy in her eyes that changed to despair as there came no answer back to her, and all around her she saw but the immovable faces of the waxen people, and the astonished ones of the crowd.

Then a curious thing happened, and one
that those present have never forgotten—
never will forget to their dying day. The
girl stood quite still, and there broke from her
lips the refrain of grand old Robert Herrick's
once famous Madrigal,

> " *Cherry ripe ! ripe, ripe I cry,*
> *True and faire ones come and buy !*
> *Come and buy . . . .*"*

Then she paused, lifted her hand, and waited
for the burden of the song to be taken up by
another pair of lips. There was not a sound
save of the distant footsteps that went to and
fro, and the muttered exclamations of the
crowd. Then she took up the verse again.

> " *If so be you ask me where*
> *They doe grow, I answer, There :*
> *Where my Julia's lips doe smile*
> *There's the land or cherry-ile !*"

Here the voice that had started so bravely
with its lilt of youth and freshness, died away
into a passionate quivering sob. . . .

" I shall lose her !" she cried, " I shall lose

* Old version of song.

her !" and the people all fell back to make way for her as she fled through the ante-chamber, and the Hall of Kings. Hindered here, jostled there, she yet reached the street entrance in time to see a carriage driving rapidly away, from the window of which there looked a girl's face, brown eyed, brown haired, fair as the day, the face of Mignon's lost sister, Muriel.

" *Muriel !* " she cried. " *Muriel !* " Hopeful and overjoyed, she dashed after her in swift pursuit.

Lost in the sea of traffic, bewildered, confused, she yet pushed blindly on. . . . There was the carriage in the distance that held her darling, and she must get to it . . . . if only these cruel carts and cabs would not come between ; if only she could pass that great ugly van before her ! The slender little figure in white made a sudden perilous dash forwards, slipped and fell. . . . The driver, occupied in chaffing a passing acquaintance, saw nothing. The horses went stolidly on. Some one, who had followed her all the way,

came from behind and caught her in his arms
—caught her from the death that in another
moment would have come to her at the hoofs
of those stolid well-fed horses.

" Let me go !" she cried, struggling fiercely
to free herself ; " do you know *what you are
doing?* I shall never find her now—*never !*
And oh ! how I *hate* you and I wish that you
were *dead !*"

CHAPTER IX.

"The pearliest dew not brings
Such morning incense from the fields of May,
As do those brighter drops that twinkling stray
From those kind eyes—the very home and haunt
Of sisterly affection."

 YOUNG man who was digging in his garden with great industry and vigour, and who sent his spadefuls of mould flying hither and thither, as though they were missiles sped after the vanishing heels of an enemy, felt all at once convinced that something unusual had happened to him. He paused in his toil, and looked around.

Something *had* happened. At the top of the garden-wall bloomed a flower that was never grown by sunshine, wind, or rain ; that had a wistful delicate face of its own, and a pair of blue eyes that looked anxiously at the gardener; that was, in short, Mignon.

Do the tears of the very young, and they to whom sorrow is a word, not a meaning, blister the eyes, and wring the heart as those shed by souls to whom misery is an established fact, misfortune a recurrent and ever-faithful guest? I trow not. To the fresh unworn heart, with its springs of emotion as yet unsounded and untouched, these early tears that seem to it so bitter, are in sooth but a novel experience that has almost the form of a luxury . . . . a timorous step or two taken into a dark and unbeautiful land, from whence it retreats with no more unquiet feeling than has he who wanders from the sunlight into the shadow, from the shadow back into the sunlight, knowing that the latter, not the former, is his home.

It is grief added to grief, nay, it is the very intensity of the memory of grief, that alone produces those scalding agonising tears that wear channels about the eyes that death itself has not power to smooth away . . . . the woes of the very young leave the eyes clear as crystal, bright as the day, and are as quickly dried as is the silver dew upon the morning grass.

Adam, throwing down his spade and looking up at that gentle apparition, discovered in her face no sign of the passionate anger and grief that had convulsed her yesterday; on the contrary, she had a timid air, and her voice was extremely low and somewhat faltering as she said :

" Adam !"

" Yes, miss."

" Would you mind very much if I were to *speak* to you ?" she said.

" To speak to me, miss ?" he said in a voice no whit more resolute than her own.

" Yes, if you do not mind."

He fetched a ladder—it looked very like a new one—pitched it against the wall, and in another moment there was but a hand's-breadth between the girl's face and his.

" I want to ask you a question," she said,

hanging her head, and looking sorely ashamed. "Supposing that you loved somebody very dearly, better than anything else upon earth, and you had lost her and were always thinking of her day and night, and longing for the time when you would find her again, to part from her never any more, and it happened one day by the strangest chance that she was quite near you, almost within reach of your hand, and you knew that if you could only get to her, the long weary waiting would be all over, and you would look into her very face, hear her very voice, and almost *die* for pure gladness that your arms were about her again, would you not for the moment *hate* any one who came between you and her, yes, and wish with all your heart that he was *dead?*"

"I should hate him," said Adam, "with all my heart."

"No," she said gently, "you would not, though in your anger you might be so wicked as to think you did; and afterwards, when you found how that person had saved your life, at the risk of his own, would you not feel so desperately sorry and ashamed of yourself that you would be quite afraid to look that person in the face ?"

He was beginning to understand the drift of her meaning now, and a sudden brightness overspread his features, that made him look a different man.

" And was it *that* you wished to say to me, Miss Mignon ?" he said ; and it was curious how different her name sounded on his lips to Prue's literal and English pronunciation of it. " Why, I thought nothing of your words —people say a great many things when they're angry that they don't mean, and I haven't given those a single thought ;" and in this he lied, for they had never ceased to ring in his ears since the time that she had uttered them.

" Have you not ?" she said joyfully ; " then that is all right, and we will forget all about it, and—would you mind *my shaking hands* with you, Adam ?"

He took her soft fair little hand in his

brown earth-stained one, looking down upon it as though he held some rare and costly gew-gaw, that was unfamiliar yet beautiful to his eyes. Then he laid it down on the wall as carefully as though he feared it might break.

"Thank you, miss," he said.

"*She* will thank you better than I ever can," she went on, "for what you have done for me; and she will scold me—ever so gently—for putting myself into that state, because I could not overtake her, for she will say, 'And if you saw me in London, might you not have been sure that I should come straight off to you at Rosemary as soon as ever I was able?' only, you see, I did not think about that, but only that she would not answer when I called her—no, nor even listen, when I sang the old song."

"*And if she can love a sister in this fashion,*" thought Adam, "*what will not her love be when her heart awakens at last to the lover and the husband?*"

She had paused in her speech, not because

she had suddenly become conscious that she
was talking too freely to the young gardener
—she was too absolutely ignorant of the
bienséances of society and the world for that
—moreover, her instincts were too pure and
good to lead her astray, or cause her to
recognise him for any other than the honest
man that he was ; but because there was passing through her mind the memory of the tender
foolish promise that she and Muriel had made
long years ago : how, if either should find
herself separated from the other, she was to
go through the world as Blondel did in
search of Richard Cœur de Lion, singing
the favourite song agreed upon between
them ; for with the song on the lips of the
one, the echo in the heart of the other, how
could they fail to find each other at last, as the
faithful Blondel sought and found *his* master ?

To their passionate, childlike faith all
things had seemed possible, and now that
the separation had indeed come, they were to
Mignon possible still . . . . though it might
be doubted if there remained to that other

lost, beloved sister one article of the simple old-world creed that had so amply sufficed to her in the far-away innocent days of her early youth.

"But now," said Mignon, heaving a deep sigh of delight, "it is all coming straight; and if she does not come to-day she will be sure to come to-morrow, and we shall be together all the rest of our lives, and, I hope, go away from here."

"You would go away from here," said Adam abruptly, "go away altogether, miss?"

"I hope so," she said gaily; "indeed, why should I stay a day longer than I am obliged, when I have nothing on earth to leave but the fowls and the raspberry and currant bushes, for of course Prue would come too?"

"You are right," he said; "you have nothing else to leave."

Something odd in his voice arrested the girl's attention.

"Would you too like to be going away?" she said. "Do you sometimes grow tired ot

gardening all the year round, as I do of my
lessons and idleness ?"

"Sometimes," he said.

"And yet it is a beautiful garden," she
said, leaning her arms upon the wall, and
gazing abroad at the trim well-kept fruit-
trees and the smart flower-garden beyond ;
"I don't think I could ever be dull with all
those flowers for companions—they always
seem to me to be far better company than
some people are !"

"Would you like a bunch, Miss Mignon ?"
he said quickly, and thinking that he saw
his way clear to an hour at least of her
society.

"Are you sure you would not be robbing
your master ?" she said doubtfully ; "of
course I should like to have them, but——"

"Then so you shall," said Adam ; "I'll
bring them over to you in less than two
minutes, miss."

And with that, the brown head disappeared
from one side of the wall, the fair one from
the other, and Mignon betook herself to the

wooden chair that had never held her in so
bright and joyous a mood as was hers to-
day.

She looked around at the homely uncared-
for garden, and found it fair and pleasant, as
the thought filled her heart, how in a few
hours perhaps Muriel's eyes would have
fallen upon it; she glanced at the fat sour
green bodies of the gooseberries, and smiled
to think that, after all her devout longings
for their fruition, it was very likely she
would not be here to eat them. And then
Adam reappeared at the top of the wall,
bearing an old mat and gardening knife in
one hand, and a great nosegay of roses in the
other.

They were every whit as sweet as though
they had been grown a hundred miles from
London town, and, as Mignon's hand closed
upon them, she saw not the four grey walls
that shut her in, but the stately terraces and
brilliant rose-gardens of her beautiful birth-
place, Silverhoe. She saw this same garden
every day, and each night before she slept

she walked in fancy all round and about it;
in the winter when the snow was on the
ground, and in the summer when it was all
green and beautiful . . . . *there* were no high
walls to shut her in, and prevent her getting
a good breath of God's air, but all was open
and free, where she could wander up and down
and in and out, and nowhere be met by bolts
and bars and other people's gardens and
houses and busy roads . . . . it had used
to be her joy to watch the seasons, and to
await the coming out of the flowers one
by one, from the first flaming velvety moss-
cup that she called her winter rose, to the
early boisterous February days when the
violet roots began to gather their scent, and
the hawthorn buds would come stealing out
like forgotten snow from the bare black stalks,
while to the laggard primroses and wind-
flowers she would stoop down and whisper:

"Come out! come out! spring is rushing
upon us, and you are all behindhand and
nothing will be ready; how will you look
then?"

And it was her foolish fancy that they came
a little the faster for her asking them, because
they knew she loved them every one, and was
so wearying for a sight of their pretty delicate
faces . . . . And Adam looked at the girl,
and there passed through his mind — and
surely it was strange that a gardener should
know aught of such matters—the lines :

> " Fold
> A rose-leaf round thy finger's taperness
> And soothe thy lips . . . ."

But aloud he said :

" As I have nothing to do this afternoon,
perhaps you will allow me to give the garden
a little weeding, miss ?"

" Oh yes," she said absently, being far too
much taken up with her treasures to particularly mind what he did, or did not do.

Having looked all about and decided that
the weeds grew thickest in the immediate
neighbourhood of Mignon, Adam deposited
his mat at a distance of about two yards from
her feet.

Setting to work in a very business-like and energetic fashion, he had presently a symmetrical row of green tufts before him, and no sound save the scrape, scrape of his knife broke the silence.

Any one coming suddenly upon the pair would have said that, over their weeds and flowers, these two people were thinking very deeply ; and so they were, only the thoughts of one were far more profound than those of the other.

" Adam," said Mignon at last, laying her roses down in her lap, " have you got a sweetheart ?"

The question was put with such perfect good faith, moreover with such absolute confidence in a serious reply, that it was equally impossible to resent, or to evade the question.

" Perhaps, miss," he said, smiling ; and it was extraordinary the difference a smile made to his face—it turned its power to sweetness, and altogether displaced a certain sternness that distinguished it ; also bringing to light one of those curious freaks of nature, a dimple, that is rarely found on a man's face unless Venus is to strongly influence his fortunes at one period or another of his life. " Why, miss ?"

" Because, if you had not," she said, lowering her voice, " I know of somebody who would just suit you—a very fine woman ; and of course you like a fine woman—do you not, Adam ?"

" Pretty well, miss," said Adam, whose taste rather inclined to the *petite* in womankind.

" And you would not mind her being a little older than yourself?" said Mignon ; " you would not consider that an *objection ?*"

" Not if I liked her," said Adam, smiling, " but I won't ask you to trouble about it on my account, miss, because"—he lifted his head and looked her full in the face—" I'm suited."

" Have you quite made up your mind?" she said, looking greatly disappointed ; " do you think she would mind very much if you married somebody else ?"

"I don't know about *her*," he said, smiling, "but *I* should mind it, miss."

"It is a great pity," said Mignon, shaking her head, "for I am sure Prue would have made you a most excellent wife ; and then, if ever I have a garden of my own, you could have been my gardener. It is certainly very provoking !"

"You forget, miss," said Adam, "that even if I liked Mrs. Prue, it's very likely she would not have liked *me*."

"Do you often write love-letters, Adam ?" said Mignon gravely.

"Maybe, miss. Why ?"

"I only wanted to know," she said, resting her chin on her hand, and her elbow on her knee, "what you would consider a *reasonable* time to elapse between the writing one and receiving a reply."

"Do you mean if I wrote to her, or *she* wrote to me, miss ?"

"If *she* wrote to *you*."

"If I liked her," said Adam, "I should answer it straight off; but if I didn't like her, I should not answer it for two or three days, or perhaps a week."

"Oh!" said Mignon, quite crestfallen. "Then, if a gentleman did not answer a person's letter straight off, you would say he did not care very much about that other person?"

She looked so wistful and lovely as she asked the question, that Adam set his teeth hard, thinking. "Can she love him—already?"

"One can't always tell, miss," he said aloud. "People go away sometimes, or are ill, or busy, or something."

"But, surely," said Mignon, "a man usually answers a first love-letter—the very first a girl ever wrote to him?"

Adam turned his head aside; he was pale as he said to himself, "Her first love-letter . . . . Mignon's first love-letter . . . . and to *him!*"

"He would be sure to answer it, miss," he said quietly, "if he received it—quite sure!"

He waited for more, but as she did not speak he went steadily on with his work, and by-and-by the girl picked up a newspaper lying by her chair, and with a little frown upon her forehead began to read.

" I *cannot* believe that," she said, after perusing a paragraph that set forth how a man, after partaking of such light and digestible nourishment as clasp-knives, shoemaker's sparables, brass-headed nails, and a few dozen or so of any other leaden and brass trifles that he had been so fortunate as to meet with, died from a slight overdose of iron filings. " Some of them *must* have stuck in his throat ; I'm sure they would have in *mine !*"

" I beg your pardon, miss," said Adam, " but did you speak ?"

" No," she said, " at least not to you. I have got into a bad habit of talking out loud. It has occurred to me once or twice that a person might almost hear what I am saying on the other side of the wall !"

Adam, intent on his weeds, blushed.

It was many years since he had done himself so much credit, for he was a cool person-
age, and not easily put out of countenance,
so that this sudden access of red-brick colour
argued a tenderness of conscience, or a freshness of feeling for which no one who was
acquainted with him would have given him
credit.

"Why, I declare," said Mignon, regarding
him attentively, "you're blushing!"

"It's the heat, miss," said Adam, throwing
back his head. "It's warm work, weeding."

He laid down his knife and stood erect, to
stretch his cramped limbs perhaps, and a
magnificent specimen of manhood he made,
with his superb *physique* and grand face—
grand by reason of its unconscious nobility of
regard and expression; the face of a man who
had long ago begun to think and feel, but who
had not yet cast the noble credulity of youth
behind him, or attained to that which has
been termed the most immoral of infidelities
—a disbelief in human nature.

But Mignon was not looking at him; her

glance had fallen upon the wheelbarrow, and
as she looked she rubbed her eyes, for instead
of being a heap of ruins, there it stood, respect-
ably upright, saying, as plain as it could speak,
" Come for a ride !"

" Have the pixies been here in the night ?"
she said, opening her blue eyes still wider, " or
have *you* ?"

" It looked untidy, miss," he said, " and so
—I mended it."

She was dying to go for a ride in the
barrow, and *he* was dying to take her one ;
but lest it should put the notion into her head
that he had already seen her, from over the
wall, enjoying that agreeable recreation, how
was he to make the proposal ?

On the other hand, was it quite compatible
with *her* dignity to do so, rather would not
this somewhat sober young man despise her
in his heart for a hoyden ?

" It's beautifully clean," said Mignon, sighing, and thinking how fast Adam's strong
arms would spin her round and round, twice
as fast as Prue's.

" There's something very handy about a barrow," said Adam reflectively; "one can carry things in it, and one can *sit* in it, and, at a pinch, why one can even take a *ride* in it; and though you wouldn't believe it, miss, a ride in a barrow is downright exciting, because, you see, there's always the chance that if you don't hold on tight you'll tumble out."

" But doesn't the wheel ever come off?" said Mignon, red at her own duplicity.

" It won't *to-day*," said Adam decidedly. " Now supposing, miss, just for once, that you were to try how you liked it?"

And with that, and forgetting, perhaps, the difference of station between them, he extended his hand with the air of a courtier. The young lady took it with an equal grace. One little foot on the ground, one in the air, and presto! she is stepping into her chariot, another moment, and she is seated,

" As beautiful as a butterfly,
    As proud as a queen,"

her lap full of roses, her eyes full of light,

flying along on what literally seem to her to be the wings of the wind !

Not for long does this mad race last; fortunately, perhaps, for Adam's legs, there comes an interruption, summary and unexpected. A door bangs violently; it is the one communicating with the other garden.

Crushing the gravel beneath his hasty footsteps, there advances to meet the flying wheelbarrow and its contents, a handsome young man.

Adam, too, as he lays down the handles of the barrow, recognises in the new-comer that graceless young *roué*, and professed lady-killer, Philip Rideout——

CHAPTER X.

"My restless spirit never could endure
To brood so long upon one luxury,
Unless it did, though fearfully, espy
A hope beyond the shadow of a dream."

ADAM, without turning his face to
Mr. Rideout, removed himself and
his mat to a remote corner of the
garden, quite out of earshot, almost out of
sight, as though he were used to playing
gooseberry every day of his life, and understood the part thoroughly.

How *mean* of him, thought Mignon, almost
in tears, to rush off like that without *offering*
to help her out, and oh! what a dreadful
thing for a grown-up person to be caught by
the first young man who had ever written her
a love-letter, riding in a wheelbarrow!

How much ankle was she showing ? Could
she clear the whole affair gracefully by one
good bound ? No, it was too late ; here he was
with, thank goodness, no laughter in his eyes,
only something that she had never seen before,
and could not therefore be expected to understand.

" Miss Ferrers—Mignon," he cried impetuously, as he bared his head before her,
while his eager eyes fastened upon, and clung
to her face, as a bee does to a blossom, " forgive this intrusion, but I have no other means
of approaching you—and I am driven mad,
reckless, by the obstacles placed in my way—
the very letter you wrote me, dear angel, was
stolen from me—snatched from my hand ere
I had read one syllable of it. Tell me," he
cried, " have you some other lover who is seeking to frustrate my hopes with you—some
one who is given to stealing letters intended
for other people, and who brings you—roses ?"

He tapped the flowers significantly with
his forefinger as he spoke, and looked at her
with angry, jealous meaning.

"Somebody stole my letter from you?" she said, almost forgetting her ridiculous position in her surprise. "Did Prue not *give* it you?"

"I took it from her by force," said Rideout grimly, "and then somebody took it from me —'twas the strangest thing imaginable, but I have my suspicions."

"Oh! what a wicked, wicked woman!" cried Mignon; "and when I asked her *every* day too, how it was that I got no reply to it!"

"And you cared so much?" cried Rideout ardently; "it was actually a source of regret that you did not hear from me again?"

"Yes," she replied gravely, "indeed it was. When I got up in the morning I used to say to myself, 'There will be a letter from *him* to-day;' and when the evening came and Prue always came back without one, I was so bitterly, bitterly disappointed!"

"You were?" he cried in a transport; "but tell me, what did you say in that dear little letter—can you remember?"

"Oh yes," said Mignon, nodding, "almost word for word, and it was a very nice one indeed. I was most particular about that, as I was afraid that if you did not like it, you would *never* write to me again !"

"Like it !" he cried, and stooped his head suddenly and pressed his burning lips against the hand that still clasped the side of the barrow.

She did not draw it away, but looked down with a kind of puzzled wonder at the faint red mark his almost rough caress had left on the soft white flesh.

He would not have found her less innocent and ignorant for worlds; yet it struck him instantly, with the jealous, unerring instinct of the real lover, that there was in her none of that sensibility to the first approaches of love that is usual in very young women . . . . the faint curiosity and vague yearning after some more exquisite experience than any that they have ever known, dimly guessed at, yet too shadowy and impalpable to be thoroughly grasped, was altogether absent in Mignon :

the chords of the beautiful instrument were dumb under the hand of the man who swept them, and he said to himself, with an angry, impatient sense of dissatisfaction, that the touch of his lips had moved her no more than those of a woman might have done.

The outcome of this thought was the relinquishment of her hand. And then it occurred to her that he might find a standing courtship rather fatiguing than otherwise, and at the same time she thought she saw a way out of the dilemma, *alias* the wheelbarrow.

" There is a three-legged stool about *somewhere*," she said, looking at him doubtfully, and wishing with all her heart that she had had a lover before, that she might by practice have ascertained whether etiquette did not demand that she should give *him* the chair, and fetch the stool for herself.

But as Mr. Rideout turned in search of the proffered seat, she was out of the wheelbarrow, and seated in her chair in a jiffey, congratulating herself on either the lack of a sense of the ridiculous, or the perfect *savoir*

faire of the new-comer that had enabled him
to manifest no surprise at all at the position
in which he found her.

" Is that your gardener ?" he said, frowning, as he discovered the soles of Adam's feet,
and the back of his head and person, as that
young man diligently pursued his avocation
of weeding in the distance.   " Can't you send
him away ?"

" Why should I do that ?" she said, wondering, and thinking that after all love-making
was not nearly so amusing as riding in a
wheelbarrow.   " I am afraid you are not very
comfortable," she added, as she saw Rideout's
efforts to arrange himself gracefully on the
extremely narrow foundations of the stool.
After all, it would have been better to have
offered him the chair.

" Thank you," said Rideout, " I am quite
comfortable; nothing could be better, I assure
you."

But for all that he made up his mind that
he would have done more wisely to stand up.
Now Adam, had he been in the same position.

would not have paused to think of whether he were sitting or standing, and if Providence had thought fit to send him a three-legged stool, would not have noticed whether he were sitting on it or a chair, which trifling matter marks the difference that existed between the two men.

"I never, never *will* forgive Prue," said Mignon, looking at him and thinking what a pity it was that his eyes were so blue, and his hair so black.

"You are angry with her," he said, leaning forward; "you were *disappointed* that you got no reply to your letter from me?"

"I was more than disappointed," said Mignon; "I *cried!*"

"You did?" he said, drawing nearer still; "you cared for me so much as that?"

"If you had no one to speak to from week's end to week's end (save Prue), and nobody to write a letter to you, and nobody (except one other person and Prue) to care two straws whether you were dead or alive, would not you be delighted, overjoyed, *proud*

at discovering that somebody not only told
somebody else he liked you very much indeed, but actually took the trouble to write
and tell you so himself?"

"Then," said Rideout passionately, "I
suppose *anybody* would have done as well—a
travelling tinker, or the butcher's boy, or anything else that had eyes to see, heart to love,
and fingers to write to you?"

"Well," said Mignon, considering, "so
long as I did not *see* him, you know, and he
spoke properly, and wrote me a good long
love-letter every day, I don't suppose it would
have signified very much. Of course I never
expected that you and I would be talking to
one another like this!"

"And I," he said dryly, "should never have
written to you had I not been resolved on
seeing you—ay, and more than once—so our
letters were written with a difference. If it
would not tax your memory too much, perhaps you will tell me what you said in this
letter?"

"O yes," she said, putting her hand to her

head, "that is to say if you will give me a
little time for recollecting; you see it was
such a difficult job, and it took such a very
long time."

"And why was it such a terrible job?" he
said, gazing at her as though his eyes could
never be sated of her dimpled, childish
beauty, the most maddening, beguiling beauty
on earth to a man of his calibre of existence.

"You see, I had never written one before,"
she said, looking rather ashamed of the con-
fession. "Let me see—I began by saying that
I was very sorry I nearly knocked you over
in the avenue, and that I would never do it
again if I could possibly help it!"

"Yes," he said, smiling in spite of himself,
"and what else?"

"That I was very much obliged to you for
writing me a love-letter; and that I hoped you
would send me another as soon as you possibly
could, for it was so dreadfully dull here!"

"Yes!"

"And I hoped you would make the next a
little *longer!*"

" Yes !"

" I think that's all. Oh! and my kind regards. I wanted to send my love, but Prue would not *hear* of it, and so——"

" *Prue* helped you to write that letter to me ?" he cried.

" Of course she did," said Mignon. " I don't know *how* I should have got on without her, two heads are better than one, you know, and I was not at all sure of saying the right thing in the right place ! So we did it together, and really, upon the whole, I think you would have liked it very much indeed !"

" No doubt," said Rideout ; " nevertheless, *upon the whole*, I will confess that I no longer regret the loss of that letter—I no longer bear malice to the thief who stole it—he is welcome to it, he may keep it, I make him a *present* of it ! In future I will get my man Coles to assist me with my letters to you ; so long as I write the signature it will not of course matter to you whether the handwriting is mine or his ?"

" I should not mind it in the least," she said sincerely ; " a letter is a letter, and if you told him what to say it would be just as good as if you had written it yourself."

He almost stamped his foot upon the gravel in his impatience.

" Is she nothing but a little coquette after all ?" he thought.

It flashed suddenly through his mind that her composure on receiving him was possibly occasioned by considerable practice in the art of receiving lovers, and thought he would have preferred her resenting his intrusion with indignation and scorn, for, man-like, he who profited by the indiscretion was the first to condemn it. A woman never yields an inch, however innocently and generously, to a man that he does not suspect her, sooner or later, of having given way in a similar manner to some man who has come earlier. It is the very refinement of the cruelty of love, it is the blade turned back against the breast of the holder, the gift heartlessly dashed into the face of the giver ; and this treachery, so

common from man to woman, is rarely, if
ever, displayed by woman to man.

With these ungenerous thoughts in his
mind, he looked keenly at her as though he
would discover if

> " In Cupid's college she had spent
> Sweet days, a lovely graduate, still unshent,
> And kept his rosy terms in idle languishment—"

but as he looked his fears died away. His
experience of woman was wide and deep
enough to have long ago taught him that
there are two kinds of innocence—the one
that is too absolutely ignorant of evil to
tremble before, or fear any man living,
therefore· has no thought of guarding itself
against a danger it does not know to exist,
and is as much a part of the possessor as the
air she breathes (and such was Mignon's);
and the purity that is pure *consciously*, with
a full knowledge of its own exceeding value,
and that may be described as the product of a
carefully cultivated and well-watched-over soil
—an innocence that is only compatible with
the clearest possible knowledge of evil, and

that enables her to meet her natural enemy, man, at every point--armed. He knew that prudishness is but another form of immodesty, and that she who is for ever balancing things proper *versus* things improper, arriving, when all deductions are made, at an outwardly modest and unassailable demeanour, inevitably loses the freshness and ingenious delicacy of her mind in the process, and is immeasurably less pure than she who, never having regarded aught but good, stands in no need of rule and precept to prevent her footsteps from straying into the mire.

And he also knew how dangerous to the owner is this latter form of innocence, to how many risks it is exposed, to what misconstruction it is liable, nay, how it may borrow the very garb of guilt, and how the world, to whom it is a mystery and a wonder (and the world hates mysteries and does not understand wonders), will hoot and decry it, reserving its approval and respect for that other marketable possession that is of itself, worldly. " Blessed are the pure in heart," says the Book. Who shall say that this same innocence, though perchance smirched, soiled, destroyed by a villany that it never could have conceived possible, does not contain, even in its ruins, elements of greatness and virtue that the earth-born, devil-sent, cowardly substitute does not, nor ever could possess ?

Coming out of his reverie, Mr. Rideout discovered that Mignon had picked up a newspaper that lay on the ground by her side, and was actually reading it.

" You seem interested," he said in a tone of pique, thereby revealing a most unheroic weakness in his character. No really wise man, who wishes to establish his empire firmly over a woman's heart, ever indulges in the luxury of showing himself piqued, for, by so doing, he places himself at a disadvantage that she is not slow to perceive, and licenses her to smile with superior wisdom at his folly, and when a woman begins to laugh at a man's humours, instead of being awed by them, it is but a losing game he plays, for do we not know that she will pardon a crime where she is merciless to a foible?

" I beg your pardon," said Mignon, putting her finger down on the paragraph she was reading, " but I caught sight of such an odd pretty name, and Lu-Lu and I always look out for all the fine names we can find for the book we are writing."

" You are writing a book?" he said, smiling, in spite of his crossness; " and pray what is it to be about?"

" Love!" said Mignon gravely. " We were afraid we should make a terrible muddle of the love scenes, as neither of us had ever had a real lover, but now it will be all right. We shall put *you* in as the hero!"

" And my letters?" inquired Rideout.

" *And* your letters!" said Mignon, " we shall copy those right off—they will look so much more real!"

" If it will be any further satisfaction to you," he said sarcastically, " I will send my portrait to be pinned on to the title-page. I don't make such a bad photograph altogether."

"Do you not?" said Mignon, looking at him doubtfully, for somehow his good looks did not please her one bit, and yet that dark, reckless face of his had been a fatal one to women, more fatal than Mignon ever dreamed of, as her careless eyes rested upon his features.

"And this name that took your fancy so much?" he said.

"La Mert. I can't quite understand—it seems a trial of some sort—" She paused in amazement as he caught the paper from her hand, his face pale and angry, while a streak of fiery red lay like a stain across his brow. His eyes fell on the paragraph, that ran as follows :

"La Mert *versus* La Mert.—Public interest in this *cause célèbre* will receive a fresh stimulus next week when the case comes on for hearing, as it is rumoured that in the course of it many painful family disclosures will be made."

"Why do your people allow you to see

such things as these?" he cried, striking the paper with his open hand; "vile records of sin and shame that they are, and utterly unfit reading for a young and innocent girl. Did you understand it—do you know what it meant—that paragraph?"

She looked at him in wonder, his excitement appeared to her so strange and unnatural . . . . what could she have said to so move him?

"No," she said, "I do not know what it means, but why should you mind if I did?"

"You have never seen or heard of that name before," he persisted, "either in a newspaper or otherwise?"

He awaited her reply with such eagerness, that one might have supposed his life depended upon it, and drew a sharp breath of relief as she answered, "Never!"

"Is it an omen?" he said to himself, crushing the paper between his restless hands; "whether it be or no, I care not—I will not turn back—pshaw! many a man goes through more than this to get his heart's desire . . . ."

" Mignon," he said aloud, " do you know why I came here to see you to-day ?"

" To ask me to write you another love-letter ?"

" No," he said, " I did not come for that. Will you try and understand me, Mignon, when I tell you that I love you, love you with a passion that I have sought to over-come, and cannot, that if conquered one moment has vanquished me the next, and against which I have ceased to struggle, for it has become a part of myself, it has entered into my very blood, and no man fights against his own life who is not mad or suicide—and I am neither. There are obstacles between us, dear angel, obstacles that " (" Good God !" he groaned to himself, " if she only knew what they are !") " will be removed ere long, and they who stand between us shall pass away like shadows ; the last, the best beloved among the rest, to return no more . . . . I swear it. . . ."

There was a wild and reckless defiance in his voice as he broke off that startled the girl.

It was as though he defied Heaven itself to stand between them, and Rideout caught her surprise as quickly as it arose.

" Do not be afraid," he said, with extraordinary tenderness of look and tone ; " to you I will be ever faithful and true, and neither grief, nor sorrow, nor shadow of sin or shame shall rest upon that lovely head. . . ."

He paused to watch the half smile that parted Mignon's exquisite lips (so may a child smile, who is pleased with the sound of the words it hears, yet comprehends nothing of their meaning), lips that were the crowning beauty of her face, and suggested all manner of passionate possibilities, and flatly contradicted her eyes, that were cold and clear, and more given to mirth and observation than the language of love—if their looks might be trusted to tell truth. When a woman's eyes and lips tell the same story, it is not difficult to decide what she will say or do at any given crisis of her life, and she will fulfil her fate with no more of effort than makes a fruit when it falls, ripened, to the earth ; but when reason, calm and critical, dwells in the eyes, and from thence keeps its watch over the impulses and vagaries of the too passionate heart as typified by the lips, then may it be foretold that there will sooner or later be fought a determined battle between the opposing forces, and that upon its issue will depend the future history of the woman's soul.

" Mignon," said Rideout impetuously, " does it seem a strange thing to you that I should love you as I do—without having exchanged a dozen words or been once before in your society—knowing nothing of you in short but what your face tells ?"

" Yes," she said promptly, " I do think it very odd—I told Prue so—just ask her if I did not say it was the *kindest*, the most outrageous, the most *extraordinary* thing I had ever heard in my life, and she could not account for it any more than I could !"

" And why should it be so kind and so extraordinary ?" he said; " has no one else ever fallen in love with you, Mignon ?"

"No one!" she said seriously, "what on earth should put such an idea into a person's head? and indeed I was very much obliged to you (as I told you in my letter); for I felt so lonely, and dull, and uncared for, just then; but now"—her face dimpled into sudden smiles—"I am afraid it is wickedly ungrateful of me, only I do not seem to care so much about it, and I do not think it would break my heart if you were never to write me another love-letter—for, to tell you a secret, somebody that I love beyond everything else in the world is coming to me, may come this minute even, or to-night, or to-morrow, and I shall be so perfectly happy, that I shall forget all about everything—everything—but that we are together—at last—that somebody and I . . . ."

He caught her hand so fiercely that she recoiled from him, and Adam, seeing the gesture from afar off, half rose, trembled, and knelt down again.

"And you told me that you *had* no lover," cried Rideout furiously, "and all the time—

all the time—" he stopped, almost choked by the violence of his emotions, the vehemence of his thoughts.

"A lover?" said Mignon, bewildered, "there is no lover—it is my sister."

"Your sister?" he cried, "forgive me, Mignon . . . ."

He turned pale as death under the relief her words afforded him.

"Yes," she said, almost in a whisper, "my beautiful lost sister . . . . for whom I have waited such a long long while, but I always knew she would come at last, and now she is coming. . . ."

In the course of Rideout's life he saw this girl many times, and under many aspects—in the day of her greatest happiness, as in that of her deepest tribulation—but he never again saw the look upon her face that he at this moment beheld . . . . without one shadow to dim the brightness of her hope, or one past experience that could embitter or make her fearful of the future, above all, with the priceless illusions of youth still upon her, there could at no period of her life come to her so radiant an outlook as this present.

In the days to come it was to recur to him, the look upon that joyous, childish face, until he became a man haunted by its gladness . . . . until it came to follow him like a curse, and burn into his heart like fire, until he nearly went mad in remembering that if he had known—O Heaven! if he had known—he might have fixed that joy of hers in her heart for ever, and so kept his soul clean of blood-guiltiness, if not of sin.

" Mignon," he said, drawing closer to the girl, " I came to tell you to-day, among other things, that I am going away, though do not fear, my sweetheart, but that I shall return to you. Then—then—listen !" he said earnestly ; " it is now a month since I first saw you, and since then I have been going through as many antics and love-sick tricks as a fool of a schoolboy in the first idiocy of his calf-love. I have astounded even myself at the depths of folly that I have sounded . . . . I have been compelled to acknowledge that a

phenomenon which I have always mocked
and derided as the most laughable absurdity
ever conceived, is in reality a *fact ;* in my own
proper person and against my will I have
proved it, Mignon. . . . Always remember
in the days to come that, however madly I
loved you, it was against my will, my conscience, my God, all——"

He suddenly ceased ; the last words seemed
to have escaped him involuntarily.

" I had heard," he went on, " of two people
falling in love at first sight, before either knew
the name of the other, before they had exchanged one syllable, before either even knew
if the other were married or single . . . .
twin souls, created for each other, now met at
last—in the self-same instant of their eyes
meeting, their souls have rushed together, the
stray halves made into one perfect whole, the
lifelong ache satisfied, the restless yearning
hearts finding rest and peace at last. I
had heard of this, and of the shame and grief
that ofttimes come after these sudden recog-
nitions of kindred souls, since for one who

finds his other self in time, there are nine hundred who meet, too late ! And as I have said, the theory amused me, for I believed in no love that was not material, in no affection that was not the result of daily acquaintance, propinquity, and familiarity. I could understand a sudden admiration at first sight, but *love*, as apart from *une passion*, I could not and did not understand until the day I saw you, and then and there, and in the very midst of a ridiculous situation that filled you with no other sense than that of amusement, I loved you, but it was unconsciously ; not until I had seen you many times, and learnt your face and manner by heart, did it suddenly dawn upon me that life would not be worth the living without you, and that win you I must and would, no matter what came between . . . . and I reckon myself a happy man in that I found you when I did, ere it was just too late. . . . Tell me," he cried ardently, " on that day did you feel yourself as irresistibly drawn to me as I did to you ? Did you recognise me as your——"

"Oh!" said Mignon, taking her hand away and placing it with its fellow over a face that had grown most suspiciously red, " I beg your pardon for interrupting you, I do indeed! And don't think me very rude, but—but I think we were *drawn together* with a vengeance! I never shall forget the blow I gave you as long as I live!"

And here she gave up the attempt to retain her gravity, and laughed so heartily as (by some process of reasoning best known to himself) to restore Adam to perfect equanimity.

"You did look so cross when we pelted round that tree," said Mignon, drying her eyes, " and as to your hat, I always thought it a *mercy* that neither of us stepped on it!"

Rideout was absolutely without that kind of humour that enables a man to smile at his own expense, thereby missing one of the keenest pleasures that poor mortal beings possess, and he looked at Mignon as though he found her impulse of mirth exceedingly foolish and ill-timed.

Here was this girl, he said to himself, for

whom he was sinning past redemption, so indifferent to the strength of his passion, so
unconscious of the convulsions that gave it
birth, that she could find for him no more and
no less than such laughter as she might give to
a love-sick whining boy, who came to her with
the tale of his foolish love upon his lips, and
the feel of a birch but freshly in his memory.

"Mignon," he said sternly, "you do not
seem to understand—you think all this an
excellent joke, and that there is no sober
earnest in it, but you will find out your mistake when I come back and fetch you away
to make you my wife."

"Your wife?" said Mignon, with a saucy
smile, that brought to life two delicious dimples in her delicate cheeks. "You are not—
you cannot be—so mad as to suppose I am
going to be *that?* Do you know how old I
am?" she added, looking at him seriously, and
pushing one of her little hands through her
rumpled *blonde* hair; "sixteen and a week,
and very little indeed for my age! Now, in
four or five years' time, perhaps, I might

11—2

think of marrying, if *she* did not mind, and would let us both live with her, but not now ! Why, it would be like *playing* at being married !"

" Come and play at it then," said Rideout just as seriously as she, " it will seem more like work after a bit."

" No, no !" she said, " you may fancy yourself in love with *me*, but no amount of the hardest fancying on earth would make me think myself in love with *you !*"

" Am I such an ugly devil that I *frighten* you ?" he cried passionately.

" No," she said, surveying him critically, " I should say you were very good-looking to a person who *admired* dark people. And though you are very nice and kind when you are not in a rage, I think, if ever I *do* marry, I should like a peaceable sort of a man, who did not worry me, though I should expect him to say, at least twice every day, ' Mignon, I *love* you.'"

" I will not worry you," he said, divided between anger and laughter, " and I will tell

you that every day, never fear, and in time
you will learn to love me, little Mignon."

" To love ?" she said dreamily, " do you
know what it is to love ? To long for some
one all and every day, to think of nothing
else upon earth, to weary after her, to feel
that until you get to that person you only live
one half, and that the worst half of your life.
That is love. How would it be possible to
love a man like that ?"

" Some day you will do so," he said, leaning
towards her with an air of pleading entreaty,
—" some day . . . . little sweetheart. . . ."

He did not know, he could not guess, how
terrible to her was to be the awakening of
love in her breast. She had turned her head
partly aside, and was looking down on her
roses, and he thought he would have given
everything he possessed on earth to be able
to put out his hand, and touch that downy
cheek and throat . . . . for as yet she possessed that exquisite softness of skin that on
a girl's face is the only equivalent to the bloom
upon a purple grape or plum, and is as easily

brushed away as it is impossible to replace
. . . . the longing, I say, was strong upon
him, but he, who had never before denied
himself his heart's desire for prayer, or love,
or scruple, forbore to take advantage of the
girl's innocence and loneliness ; he had indeed
sworn that until he was free to ask her to be
his wife, he would neither seek to obtain, or
wrest from her, any one of a lover's privileges.

" Mignon," he said, " I want you to listen
to me, and to try and understand me if you
can. . . . You do not love me now; it is not
possible that you should do so (for although
you seem most familiar to me since I have
watched and followed you so long, yet I have
been to you no more than any one of the idle,
impertinent young men who have stared at
you in church and out walking), but you will
be no such inapt pupil, my flower, and whether
you love me or no, you shall be no man's wife
but mine—I swear it ! And if by any cheat
or fraud any man come between us, I will
wrest you from him, ay ! and keep you, for
to no other man can you be what you are to

me, and if by any cursed misfortune I lost you, I would search the world through and through until I had found you, so do not dream that you will escape or elude me, Mignon, for you will not. In about a fortnight —you may look for me at any moment after the fourteenth day has passed—I shall return. I shall walk straight to this garden, and probably I shall find you sitting here on this old chair, and maybe you will wear a white gown and a red rose at your breast, just as you wear to-day, and you will look just as little, and childish, and lovely as you do to-day, and I shall say to you, ' Mignon, I have come to ask you to be my wife,' and you will put your little hand in mine . . . . and then, Mignon, then, in this dull old garden I will teach you one by one the lessons of *love* . . . .

" It is possible," he went on, " that people will tell you stories about me, but you will not believe them, my little one ; you will just say to yourself, ' *He is coming back in fourteen days to marry me, and he loves me dearly, dearly !*' and so you need not mind the stories.

And do not let any one fall in love with you, do not dare. . . ."

His blue eyes had so fierce a menace in them, that they appeared almost black for the moment ; then, as they dwelt on Mignon's dimpled, charming face, he smiled . . . . and so with a last long look, and a close, strong hand-clasp, he was gone.

CHAPTER XI.

" He ne'er is crowned
With immortality who fears to follow
Where airy voices lead."

SILENCE in the garden for the space of a full minute. Even the scraping of Adam's knife ceased, and turning half round he leaned his hand upon the gravel, and looked across at the girl's downcast face and lips pursed into the semblance of a pout.

Glancing up suddenly and meeting his eyes, for so intense was his regard that he could not instantly withdraw it, an idea came into her head, and jumping up she crossed the garden and came to his side.

"Adam," she said seriously, " would you

mind telling me—as you have got a sweetheart of your own, and of course know something about such matters—whether you ever
heard of a person being married straight off
against her will, whether she would or no ?"

"Such things used to be, miss," he said,
"but nowadays it's not often heard of."

"Then," said Mignon, "you would say
that if a person were threatened with such a
thing she need not be very uneasy—he could
not *make* her say ' yes ' ?"

"No," said Adam, "but she might change
her mind, or he might coax her into saying it
—you're quite sure it *would* be against her
will ?"

His keen eyes studied every line of her
face as he spoke.

"*Quite* sure !" said Mignon emphatically.
"You see, Adam, a love-letter is a perfectly
charming thing, and to know that somebody
is in love with a person is more charming
still, but what on earth would one do with a
husband ?"

"What indeed ?" said Adam, his heart as

light as a feather (and why should this be ?),
" if she is quite sure."

He was standing up now, and all homely
as was his garb, his grand comeliness made
him more than a match for the girl, who
stood with cheeks flushed by excitement
and the exceeding heat, soft hair sadly
tumbled, and partially hanging down her
back, and two red lips just parting to
speak.

" She is *quite* sure," said Mignon, nodding,
" and I am very much obliged to you, Adam.
I should not have had to ask, if Prue had got
a sweetheart, and knew more about such
matters—only, you see, she used to have one,
but has not now, poor thing !"

Then she smelled her roses, appeared to
forget all about Adam, stood still for some
moments, thinking, moved slowly away, and
presently left the garden.

He went quietly on with his weeding for
a quarter of an hour, twenty minutes, thirty,
then made up his mind that she was not
coming out again until the evening, and pre-

pared for departure.   He collected the weeds
into a respectable heap, rose, picked up his
mat, and was turning towards the ladder,
when the sound of approaching footsteps set
his heart beating, and turned his head in the
direction of the garden door.   A half smile
came over his face as he discovered not
Mignon, but Prue.

"And now," said he to himself, "the
deluge!"

He wore no hat, his face was clear as the
day before her eyes, the recognition was,
on both sides, perfect.

"You villain!" she cried, coming over to
him like a whirlwind. *"And what have you
done with that letter you stole?"*

He touched his breast. "I have it here,"
he said.

She looked down at the knife and mat he
held in his hands, at his unmistakable gardener's dress, at his shirt-sleeves and bare
head, then—

"Good Lord!" she cried, drawing the
deepest breath she ever took in her life, "and

I took you—I actually took you that night for a—gentleman !"

" And why did you ?" he said. " I don't remember giving you any particulars as to my station in life. I told you I was an honest man—which I am."

" An honest man !" retorted Prue, with intense scorn, " and you have the impudence to call yourself *that ?* And pray, if I may make so bold as to ask the question, what have my young lady done to you that you should take such a powerful interest in her as to *steal her letters ?*"

" The question *is* a bold one," said Adam, " and one that I don't choose to answer any one but—*herself.*"

" You'll have the face to tell her what you've done ?" said Prue, altogether staggered by his assurance.

" Yes, I shall tell her."

" No wonder you disappeared so quick that day at Madam Tussore's," she said. " No wonder I'd scarcely got sight of my young lady than you bolted——"

She paused, for the first time remembering that this man, no matter what his previous misdeeds might be, had saved her young mistress's life at the peril of his own.

But as she looked at him, cool, confident, fearless, her anger rose again and burned hotly in her breast.

"And if you're going to tell her," she said, "why didn't you do it before? you've had opportunities enough while you've been sneaking about her garden, goodness knows!"

"I did not intend to tell her that until I thought it time to tell her — other things."

"Do you know what you are *talking* about?" cried Prue, in a fury, "that you speak of telling her this and that, as though she was a cook or a housemaid—one of your own class—do you know who she *is*, I say?"

"A young woman," said Adam, his face softening, "and a good one too—God bless her!"

Prue's anger suddenly left her, it was too useless to be retained, and she looked at the young man with a sensation of despair. As yet not the dimmest suspicion of the heights to which his audacious hopes aspired had shadowed itself ever so faintly upon her mind.

" 'Tis a true saying that ill-doings never prosper," said Prue, "and I'm sure yours didn't. You stole the letter and made a thief of yourself—for nothing. You tried to keep Mr. Rideout and my young lady apart—well, he's mad in love with her, and ready to marry her whenever she pleases. There !"

" Yes," said Adam, " I know it. He was here this afternoon."

" *Here,*" cried Prue, starting back, " *here,* did you say ?"

" Yes, why not ? Has she not told you ?"

" I've not seen her. *He's* a bold one," she added half aloud, " to cut in like that the very first time I turned my back !"

" But I don't think your mistress will marry Mr. Rideout," said Adam.

" And why not ?" said Prue tartly, " unless you're going to take upon yourself to forbid the banns ?"

" There are one or two objections," said Adam calmly, " or at least—I think so."

" And what may they be ?" cried Prue, angry and inquisitive ; " maybe you think she's over-young for marrying ?"

" No," he said, " I should not consider that an objection. Plenty of girls marry as young as she."

" Or he's poor ?"

" He is very rich—as riches go."

" Maybe he's not his own master ?"

" He has no parents, and is absolutely his own master."

" Then," said Prue, " if he is rich, and his own master, and so deep in love with her, and if she favours him, whatever on earth can there be to keep them apart ?"

"Two things," said Adam. "In the first place, Mr. Rideout is married already ; and in the second, I mean to marry her myself."

CHAPTER XII.

"Ha! ha! the wooing o't!"

WAS that Mignon who sat so still and quiet on the old wooden chair, the neglected "Goblins" by her side, her untouched work stretched in a forlorn strip at her feet?

Some one who watched her said to himself that she looked as though a blight had already fallen upon her, and he shook his head so sadly that the wallflowers trembled and shook also.

Such a merry little soul as she used to be, he said to himself; such a joyous, happy, bewitching little hoyden!

What could he do to amuse her? To go

over he was forbidden, to speak to her even he dared not, but no one could prevent him from *looking*, and he had made no promises about messages without words. A thought struck him !

He rapidly descended his ladder, disappeared, presently became visible again bearing a small basket lined with leaves, and apparently filled with something delectable. He attached to this basket two stout cords of considerable length, then mounted the ladder, carefully placed the basket on the top of the wall, adjusted the cords, and proceeded to lower it gently into the garden beneath.

Bibbety bob—bob—bob—down they came, so gently as not to disturb a single leaf, and so noiselessly, that not until they were almost on a level with Mignon's head did she discover them.

Cherries ! round, shining, rosy, red ! As she looked at them her eyes brightened, she could almost feel her teeth meeting in their soft, luscious, plump sides . . . but were they for her ? though if not, then for whom else ?

All at once she burst into a peal of laughter, and clapped her hands.

"Adam!" she said, "why *of course* it's Adam!" but on directing her glance upwards, she found no Adam, only a group of wall-flowers.

Her eyes reverted to the basket. It had paused in its descent to a convenient distance from her hand, and now gave a gentle bob or two of invitation, as much as to say, "Come, come, you are very backward; why don't you eat me?"

She could resist the temptation no longer, but put out a little eager curved hand, and incontinently a cherry was down her throat! It is only the first step that costs, the rest was easy enough; in two minutes the basket was empty!

This fact appeared to give it satisfaction; for it executed various hops and skips of a jubilant character, finally whisking itself out of sight in an ecstasy of bobs that suggested "Good-bye, and thank you!"

Mignon sat quite still, surrounded by cherry

stones, her blue eyes gradually travelling upwards and after the basket, then she sighed, looked at her cherry-stained fingers, shook her head, blushed. "You are a greedy little pig," she said, "but oh ! how I wish it had all got to come over again !"

She curled her two red lips, the one over the other, as though she tasted those cherries still, then looked about for the ladder that she might by means of it convey her gratitude to the young gardener; but alas! it was no-where to be found. He had apparently taken it home again.

"Flowerpots are no good," she said, gravely; "they always give way under one, besides one would want *dozens*. I'll thank him for them to-morrow !"

Then she sighed and went away ; but to-morrow came, and yet another morrow, and Mignon was not found in her old place ; and Adam, watching all day long for her, fell to asking himself, had Prue, with all the inca-pacity of a woman for keeping a secret, told her young mistress everything, and was she

too proud and angry to so much as walk in the
garden, where she would be subjected to the
chance of his appearance ?   When the third
day had come, and brought no Mignon, he
made up his mind that Prue had betrayed
him, and girding up his loins, prepared himself for as disagreeable a duty and scene, as
a man and a lover with any pride and self-
respect ever undertook.

CHAPTER XIII.

"I loved her to the very white of truth
And she would not conceive it."

LEANING her brows against the window-pane in the bare and now deserted schoolroom, Mignon kept her watch for Muriel, and felt her soul die within her for longing to see the well-known slender figure turn in at the garden gate, to hear the echo of her hurrying feet upon the gravel walk, and the sound of her loving eager cry of "Gabrielle! Gabrielle!" Three days had gone by since Mignon had, in mere idleness of spirit, paid that visit to Madame Tussaud's that was fated to end in so strange a fashion; three days . . . . only three, no more than an hour to untroubled happy people, yet a

long, long while to this girl who had for the
first time tasted the exceeding bitterness of
that hope deferred which " maketh the heart
sick."

The silence of her sister for the past year
and a half had been hard to bear, but the
treasure and reward lying in the future had
been anticipated with such entire trust, that
though in the earlier portion of the time she
had suffered keenly, yet she had never once
endured the misery of either doubt or despair.   But now, now that she knew Muriel
to be close at hand, divided from her merely
by a few houses, and fields, and roads, and
conscious (as she must be) of how anxiously
the little sister was watching for her coming,
yet making no sign, sending no word, seeming to forget her, as though she had no
existence, now, I say, upon Mignon's loving
and faithful heart fell the cold and cruel
blight of open and acknowledged neglect.
Neglect . . . . that is more pitiless than
jealousy, more inhuman than hatred, that
(even as the plant that entangles and crushes

the life out of the living insect it enfolds) closes about the heart with a numbing embrace that slowly destroys all energy, hope, and gladness, yea, and that better part of the existence without which we are happier dead than living.

To suffer and sorrow for misfortune's sake is natural and healthy, to receive unkindness from the world is easy and light to bear, but neglect at the hand of one from whom love alone is due (else should we not mourn its withdrawal so deeply) is unnatural, and a violation of the laws of human nature. And this thing, that uses no harsh words, acts no tangible savagery, that has even an outward seeming of fairness and gentleness, and is liable to no such punishment as is meted out to bold and overt forms of cruelty, is yet the most dastardly and barbarous of all the weapons placed in our hands whereby we have power to stab the hearts of those who love us. The shadows were beginning to creep about the girl's young life—to creep higher and higher till they rested upon her heart and settled there, but this she could not know as she watched patiently on from day to day, and hour to hour, for one who never came.

Some one came from behind her, and took one of the soft girlish hands between her two hard rough ones.   It was Prue.

"Miss Mignon, dear heart," she said, "and won't you come out for a bit this afternoon, even if 'tis only so far as the garden? You've not crossed the threshold these three days, and you so used to pretty nigh live in the open air!   And if *she* should come"— the woman hesitated and turned aside— "couldn't I fetch you in less than a minute?"

"And what would *she* say," cried the girl, "if I were not here to run out to the door and welcome her? She would think that I was angry with her, that I had grown *careless* of her"—she paused, and put both her hands suddenly to her side. "Such a pain, Prue!" she said, "oh! such a pain! Such a feeling that everything is going *wrong* with me, and that I don't know how to put it right again ! If I had not seen her, if I did not *know* that she was alive and well, I should think that it meant that she was *dead !*"

" No, no, miss," said Prue gently, " not dead—forgetful maybe, but not dead. Don't ever think of such a thing, little mistress ; and why should you fret yourself so sore for one as never seems to fret herself about you ?"

" You do not understand," said Mignon coldly and proudly, and turned without another word and went quietly away.

She paused a moment upon the threshold of the house-door, for her eyes were dazzled by the sun, and the vivid green of the trees and bushes smote her almost painfully after the subdued light within doors ; then she descended the steps and went round soberly enough into the garden. It seemed to her a long while since she had walked in it, and that a great deal had happened to her in that time, although in truth nothing new had come to her save the sharpness of a disappointment that to her undisciplined heart had all the force of a revelation, and the cruelty of an injustice.

She sat down in the old place and picked up her embroidery, that lay just where she had left it, the complexion thereof being in no way improved by the night dews and noonday sun. There had not been a drop of rain, so the needle was still unrusted and filled with cotton ; a thimble lay in her pocket, she drew it out and commenced working. The unquiet mind is an excellent incentive to manual labour : she had never before worked so steadily and industriously as she did now. Somebody came through the door communicating with the other garden and advanced towards her, but she did not lift her eyes ; she believed it to be Prue, and she was angry with the woman, and did not desire either her society or her conversation. But when the steps paused before her, she knew that it was not Prue, and looking up, saw that it was Adam the gardener.

" Is that you, Adam ?" she said, surprised that he should have come by way of the garden instead of the wall, "and have you come to do some weeding for me to-day ?"

" No," he said, " not to-day."

Something in his voice made Mignon glance at him in surprise. Was this *Adam*, this man with boldly-lifted brows and fearless regard, as of equal meeting equal, yet with some feeling stronger and deeper than pride subduing and softening his features to a nobility that she had never seen them wear before ?

Scarcely noting his expression, she became cognisant of an indefinable yet certain change in his manner. Altogether innocent of the intense vulgarity that passes by the name of high breeding, and that would regulate politeness by the position occupied by the person addressed in the social scale, that is for ever drawing distinctions, and measuring people not by what they *are*, but by what they have, Mignon possessed that sweet and gentle courtesy that is inbred in some men

and women, and put forth as naturally to the
poor as to the rich ; but at the first suspicion
of an encroachment, by either look or word,
the proud Ferrers blood showed itself, and
her tone instantly defined his position as
gardener, hers as gentlewoman, as she said :

" You wish then to speak to me ?"

" I have something of yours in my possession that I wish to restore to you," he
said, and drew from his pocket a letter sealed
with red wax.

She took it from his hand and read aloud :

" PHILIP RIDEOUT, ESQ.,
                    Lilytown."

The handwriting was her own. The
matter of the lost letter had concerned her
but little, nay, in the trouble of the last few
days, she had forgotten its very existence,
and the time of her writing it seemed a long,
long while ago to her now.

" How did you come by this ?" she said,
in wonder ; " where on earth did you find
it ?"

"I stole it from Mr. Rideout," said Adam.

"You stole it!" she said, staring at him in utter bewilderment, "and why did you do that?"

He made no reply, only bent his eyes downwards, and waited quietly for her next words.

She passed her hand hastily over her brow, looked at the letter, then back again at him. Then, even as it had done to Prue, the indifference, or, as it seemed to her, effrontery, of his bearing angered her.

"And so you were a thief all the while," she said slowly, "and I thought you were an honest man! Who gave you the right to intermeddle in my affairs? What was it to you whether I wrote to Mr. Rideout, or no? Did Miss Sorel set you over me as a *spy* and a keeper when she went away?"

No answer.

"So *that* was why you came into the garden that morning?" she cried, roused more and more by his apparent apathy, and with all her other troubles swept clean away in the excitement of the moment.

"I saw you peeping into my book and fingering my thimble, were you trying to find a clue to my other doings ? Were you trying to *pick up* something to my discredit ?"

No answer.

"I have only one more question to ask you," she went on; "*why did you not read my letter* while you were about it—why do you return it to me now, above all, with the seal unbroken ? Better an out-and-out dishonour than one badly cloaked with a semblance of truth !"

Still no reply, not a tremor of the eyelids, not a quiver of the firm lips, to show that her barbed words struck home, and wounded him to the quick.

"And if you thought to do harm by stealing that letter," she said, with a triumphant ring in her voice that dashed out the scorn, "you did not—it made no difference to Mr. Rideout, he came and told

me all about it! But you know that already
—you were in the garden *spying* when he
came, though surely you made a terrible
mistake in being *out of earshot!* You might
have come as near as you pleased, and it
would never have occurred to me that you
were listening—for, you see, I did not know
you were a *spy.* And now I understand why
I caught you staring so at me when he went
away .... Tell me!" she cried, "if you are
man enough to be able to speak the truth,
who set you to watch me, to lie in wait for
my letters, to come into my garden on false
pretences, to lead me on to talk to you *trust-
fully* as I should to Prue? Was it—though
I *cannot* believe it—Miss Sorel?"

"No," he said, "it was not Miss Sorel."

"You did it simply and solely of your own
accord?"

"Simply and solely of my own accord!"

"I have no more to say to you," she said,
"except that I am sorry—very sorry—that
I have found you out to be so bad."

Her eyes were wistful, her face was pale

. . . . following upon the broken promise of
the past three days came this new disappointment, for she had liked and instinctively
trusted this man, and she was, as she had
said, *sorry.*

His heart ached as he looked at her, and
to himself he said that his punishment was
beginning . . . .

"And now," he said aloud, " you will
listen to me. Had you not better sit down ?
you will be tired."

She looked at him, hesitated, then sat
down again, obeying the law that impels
the strong will to yield to the stronger—
a submission that has in it all the elements of rebellion, and is as little grateful to the recipient as it is hateful to the
giver.

" You have called me thief, eavesdropper,
and spy," he said, " and each of those appel-
lations is justly bestowed upon me, but you
have not yet discovered the full extent of the
fraud I have practised upon you. Can you
guess what that is ?"

She looked at him, measuring him from head to foot, his common dress, his pride of regard, his well-shaped feet and hands, and all at once something flashed upon her that she had been blind indeed not to have discovered long ago, and catching that sudden light in her eyes, Adam knew that she had guessed the truth.

"You are not a gardener after all," she said, "you are a gentleman! And you came into my garden pretending to be what you were not?" she said slowly. "You obtained a footing in it by a lie, and kept it by hundreds of others?"

"Yes," he said, but by now a red flush had crept slowly up to his brow and settled there.

"You let me order you about as though you were a servant, and laughed at me in your sleeve, while you weeded the gravel walks?"

"I let you order me about, but I did not laugh at you in my sleeve."

13—2

" I gave you half a crown !"

" Yes !"

" And I let you wheel me in a wheelbarrow !"

" Yes !"

" And you called me *miss*."

" I did."

" And I recommended you to study English history !"

" Yes."

" And you sent me cherries over the wall, and I ate them—*every one!*"

" Yes !"

" Oh !" cried the girl, starting up and covering her scarlet cheeks with both hands, " I shall never get over it—I shall die of shame, and oh ! sir, how I scorn, how I *detest* you !"

" Mignon," cried the young man in his excitement, and so shaken was she by the violence of the conflicting emotions that swayed her, that she never observed the slip, " I have told you the end of the story—the beginning you have yet to learn—my actions you know, but the motives that prompted them you do not——"

"Nor do I wish to hear them," cried the girl; "your actions are enough, and more than enough for me! Did you think because I was a poor friendless schoolgirl, with no father or mother, or brother—*nobody* to stand up for me—that you could play off as many *practical jokes* upon me as you pleased?"

"Mignon," cried Adam in despair, "can't you understand why I have done all this? do you not see how I have tried to be your friend all along, even if I did make a terrible mistake at the beginning?"

She did not reply, she was weeping; a great many causes had conspired to make the salt fountain overflow; but Adam took those tears (being ignorant of the pressure of other troubles upon her) to be altogether due to his own bad behaviour.

"Mignon," he cried again, distracted by the sight of them, his calmness utterly forsaking him, "won't you try to overlook the past—won't you begin it all over again, on a

better, surer foundation, won't you give me
at least the chance of *earning* your good
opinion ?"

"How could I trust you again ?" she said,
taking her hands away from her face. "How
should I know when you were telling me
truth, and when falsehood ? I *liked* you . . . .
and you saved my life," she added, sobbing,
" I can never forget *that*——"

" If it will soften your anger to me," he
said gently, "remember that, and forget all
the rest . . . . you need fear no intrusion
from me, or that I shall molest you in any
way, and you may walk in your garden with
as much security as though I were a hundred
miles away.   I will never enter it again, *until
you call me.* If you should require a friend
at any time send for me ; a man may be a
good friend, Mignon, although he be liar,
thief, spy, and eavesdropper.   Prue has
somewhat to say to you on the subject of
Mr. Rideout that will demand your careful
attention ; and if you can ever feel that you
forgive me, will you send me one word—only

one, and you will make the most miserable man upon earth the happiest . . . ."

Then, as she made no sign, he went slowly away, and left her standing there alone.

CHAPTER XIV.

"Let the white death sit on thy cheek for ever,
We'll ne'er come there again."

"TRUE," said Mignon, sitting down unexpectedly on the floor, "I will *never* believe in anybody living again (except Muriel); and if you were to take it into your head to kill me one night in my sleep, I should not be in the *least* astonished, indeed I should say it was *exactly* what I had expected?"

"I don't s'pose you'd say anything at all in that case, Miss Mignon," said Prue, who was giving the drawing-room a thorough good dusting in anticipation of Miss Sorel's return.

"I am a very little more than sixteen

years old," said Mignon, addressing a bunch
of flowers painted by her own hand, and duly
framed and hung up on the opposite wall,
and of which the roses were so deeply red,
the violets so intensely blue, and the leaves
so overpoweringly green, that they made the
eyes wink again to look at them; "and I
think the world a shockingly wicked, deceitful,
surprising place, and human nature as bad as
bad can be. Now what should you suppose
will be my opinion of the same by the time I
am *sixty?*"

"A deal more favourable to human natur',"
said Prue, who was dusting the chaste Diana,
with averted eyes, as much as to say that if
that misguided young person fancied herself
without any clothes, *she* for one was not going
to abet the iniquity by looking at her.
"When people get a better knowledge of
theirselves, miss (and years give 'em that),
they discover so much wickedness in theirselves, that they're in no hurry to cast stones
at their neighbours. 'Tis only the young,
miss, as comes to conclusions so mighty quick,.

and finds hard words so much easier to their tongues than kind ones."

"But surely," cried Mignon, pushing back her hair, "downright wicked things, like deceit, lies, and worse, *require* hard language? Can being old turn black things into white? Do old people have an upside-down dictionary, and call virtue *vice*, and vice *virtue?*"

"No, Miss Mignon, but they go deeper than just outsides—they see reasons."

"Would any amount of reasons make it right for you to deceive me as you did about that letter, Prue? Would an old person find a satisfactory reason why Mr. Rideout should ask me to marry him, when he had a wife all the time, and his name was not Rideout at all?"

"No," said Prue, "I've got no reasons for *him*—he's a rascal—and I should like" (making a movement of her hand that in a man would have taken the form of a doubled-up fist) "to tell him so to his face."

"I can't say I am very sorry at *his* bad behaviour," said Mignon, sighing; "for I

have been racking my brains as to what good
excuse I should give him when he came back
for not marrying him, for he is such a tre-
mendous person that it would *not* be easy to
say 'No' to him; but *now* I shall just be
able to drop him a courtesy, and say, 'Thank
you very much, but does the English law
permit a person to have *two* wives?'"

"Villain!" cried Prue, "and what a silly,
believing woman was I, good Lord!"

"Perhaps it is not true after all," said
Mignon. "How are we to know that Adam
was not telling us some more stories? Though
why it should matter to *him* whether Mr.
Rideout is married or single, or what on earth
could have induced him to steal that letter, is
more than I can understand! Do you think
it is possible that he is a kleptomaniac,
Prue?"

"What's that, miss?"

"A man who appropriates other people's
goods: if he is rich, and in no want of the
things he takes, he is called a kleptomaniac;
but if he is a poor, despairing man, with a

starving wife and family at home, he is called—a thief."

" *No*, miss," said Prue, frowning; " he's not that. It wasn't stealing neither, for he give it back to you ; and when he took it, 'twas for *your good*."

"But why concern himself about my good?" said Mignon, looking puzzled. " What could it matter to him whether I wrote to Mr. Rideout, or no ?"

" Because," said the woman, " he knew you had no relations, nobody to look after you but a silly creature called **Prue**—and that Mr. Rideout was a bad man, not fit for a young lady to be writing to, and so he took the letter."

" You seem to have a very good opinion of him," said Mignon, " though I'm sure I can't see what he has done to deserve it ! The only difference between them that *I* can see is, that one came in at the garden door and made unlawful love, and the other came over the garden wall and played the spy—and really I don't think there is a pin to choose between them ! Though after all," she added, "what does it matter how they behave, what does *anything* matter, so long as *she* still delays to come, and when she must know, too, how I am wearying for her ?"

Rat-tat ! went the knocker of the hall-door, as though in answer to Mignon's words, causing her to start violently. What is there in the sound of the postman's knock that sets more hearts beating and nerves fluttering than any other sound upon earth ?

"A letter from Muriel !" she thought rather than spoke, and sprang to her feet. In a moment she had flung the house-door wide, to discover a boy on the step who handed a yellow envelope to her with the customary inquiry of " Any answer ?"

She did not hear him . . . . she was looking at the ugly narrow envelope with the most intense joy; it was from Muriel, she was sure of that, to say she was coming immediately . . . . and yet her fingers tarried, and did not seem able to open it.

Prue came out. The boy went away.

Mignon desperately tore the envelope asunder, and read aloud the following words :

From   *To*

M. GIRARDIN,   Miss GABRIELLE FERRERS,

Hôtel de B——,   Rosemary,

Paris.   Lilytown.

" An Englishwoman, named Sorel, died here suddenly last night. By examination of papers have discovered above address. Some relative must come over at once to identify body and arrange for burial."

The telegram fell from Mignon's hands. The shock, following on her triumphant and mistaken gladness, was cruel. . . . . She looked at Prue, who seemed turned to stone, and did not utter a syllable. The cook appeared in the hall, attracted thither by the instinct that invariably draws people to the scene of a catastrophe, or the place where one is in process of being announced.

" Mistress is dead !" said Prue, and threw her apron over her head.

" Dead !" said the cook, looking shocked,

but putting on the pleasurable air of excitement that domestic misfortune ever seems to
afford the ordinary, unattached servant, to
whom a death or a wedding are equally
productive of fuss and importance, agreeably
combined with a total disregard of the every-
day duties that it has been their custom to
fulfil. Mignon did not weep . . . . there
was a strange tightness about her heart, and
she felt as one who has been stunned by a
heavy and unexpected blow. She had given
the dead woman respect, not love, yet respect
is as good a thing as love in its way, and
Miss Sorel had been her only friend, save
Prue, for four long years . . . . it smote her
now with a dull and bitter pang, how often
lately she had taken her name between her
lips, carelessly, ignorantly, speaking lightly
of that home-coming that should never come
to pass . . . . at the very time, perhaps,
when *she* had been passing away to that
unutterable mystery and greeting that mortal
eye hath not seen, nor ear heard.

"The telegram said that somebody must

go," said Prue, taking her apron from her eyes. "Oh! poor mistress . . . . poor mistress .. . . . nobody ever came to see her but her brother, and he lives somewhere in the north; did she ever tell you his address, Miss Mignon?"

"Never," said the girl, and shivered, scarcely knowing why, as she recalled the sinister-faced man who had looked at her so strangely, and spoken to her so roughly, on the sole occasion when she had found herself in his presence.

"If the address is anywhere, 'twill be in the big writing-table in her room," said Prue, lowering her voice involuntarily as she uttered the pronoun that now stood for what *was not*.

"We will go and see," said Mignon, who felt as one who moves in a dream, yet knows the awaking will surely come by-and-by.

They went upstairs, and into the pretty sunny chamber that would receive its mistress never any more; treading softly, as though she were by to hear them, and looking about with that fearful awe that ever attends the dwelling-places of those who were once of us but are now apart.

The table was securely locked, and would yield to no key that the house afforded, finally, and with a roughness that made Mignon turn her head, half expecting to see the tall slender shape and the grey gown of the woman whose secrets were so rudely violated, the desk was forced open, and its orderly contents became visible. Neatly labelled packets of bills, files of accounts, school and tradesmen's books, all the tidy odds and ends of a careful manager and a prim old maid, and Prue, who had seen it all many times before, felt her eyes fill again.

The search was not a long one. Two or three slender packets of letters, indorsed "Silas Sorel to Marie Sorel," were placed in such fashion, that the most casual glance could not fail to fall upon them. Mignon drew out one of the sheets, and, turning to the heading, read :

"The How, Northallerton, Yorkshire."

As she laid the letter down again, she perceived a packet addressed to herself, and indorsed, " Not to be opened until after my death."

She took it in her hand, and again, burning summer day though it was, she shivered, and her face was very pale as she said to Prue—

" See, this is addressed to me. It is no theft to take what is my own ?"

" It is yours," said Prue, sobbing, " since she is dead. Poor soul ! poor soul !"

Five minutes later Mignon was sitting in her chamber, the unopened letter in her hand, alone.

CHAPTER XV.

"I am for the house with the narrow gate, which I take to be too little for pomp to enter; some that humble themselves may, but the many will be too chill and tender: and they'll be for the flow'ry way that leads to the broad gate and the great fire."

MIGNON broke the seal, and took out two enclosures, the one a long and closely-written letter, the other a sealed envelope, also addressed to herself, the superscription of which was as follows:

"*Not to be opened until the other letter is read.*"

The habit of obedience was still strong upon her; she laid it down on her lap and took up the other   It ran thus:

" In the event of my sudden decease by sick-
ness, railway accident, fire, or any one of those
urgent summonses of God that men mis-name
chance, I write these words for your enlighten-
ment and guidance, my poor little Mignon,
since, when I am gone, there will not be in the
whole world a more lonely, friendless creature
than yourself. For my own sake I do not
fear Death ; nay, I listen for his footsteps in
the stillness of the night, in the glory of the
noonday, at evening-tide when the night is
closing in, and, when he lays his cold hand
on mine, I shall go to him as gladly as a
bride to her bridegroom ; but my heart aches
when I think of you, whom I cannot choose
but leave desolate and unprovided for, and for
your sake I would live yet a few years longer,
until I had seen you placed securely beyond
the storms and temptations of life. Then I
could face your father without fear in the
Great Beyond, where he awaits me, and say
to him, ' I have left her safe, the little
daughter that you entrusted to my care . . .'
It may be that you will never read these

lines ; that I shall tell you my story some
night when the darkness hides from me your
face—the face that is a birthright from your
dead father, and yet bears a strong resem-
blance to your mother . . . that same resem-
blance to her that hardened my heart against
you, and made my looks and ways so cold to
you always.

"Thirty years ago I was but a very little
older than you now are, and happy . . . . no
bird rioting in his short summer-day gladness
was happier than I, for my heart was filled
with the first rapture and glory of a young
girl's love, than which there can on earth be
nothing more exquisite, for believe me, child,
when I tell you that, no matter how strong,
and deep, and true, may be the second love of
a man or woman, it can never approach that
first matchless passion when the fancy flew
like an arrow, and the heart followed after,
and there was no question of measure or comparison, but each poured out the riches of the
soul in one supreme gift, recking not if the
cup were drained, the golden wine squandered

in a draught, and no drop left remaining for
the long, long years of the future.

"We were but a month from our wedding-
day, your father and I, when your mother
crossed our path—beautiful, cold, unscrupu-
lous—a woman of no passions and many
vices, who lied, and schemed, and plotted, and
divided us from each other—divided us so
utterly, that to the day of his death he never
knew but that I had played him false, yet
loved me so faithfully, so enduringly, that the
last letter his poor stiffening fingers penned
was to me, as the last name he uttered, when
he lay a-dying, was '*Marie! Marie!*' not his
wife's name, only his poor lost sweetheart's.
I received and read his letter; I have it still,
it has lain ever since on my breast by night
and day, it will go with me to my coffin; and
in this letter he prayed me, for the sake of
the love I had once borne him, to befriend his
little daughter when he was gone. A ruined
man, the splendid fortune for which your
mother had married him, squandered in mad
extravagance, he knew of no one to whom he

could make such a request but me. Muriel
was old enough to earn her bread, but you
were only a child; and having made his
prayer to me, he died, and I did not shed one
tear for him, for he seemed nearer to me
dead than he had for long years been to me
living.

"He was scarcely cold in his grave when
your mother died, of a broken heart, the world
said, and the world was right; the loss of
wealth, station, and all that was to her the
very principle of existence, killed her. She
was no more than a shadow to Muriel and
you, and when she went, you scarcely missed
her, your lives were literally bound up in
each other, and for even your rarely-seen
father you had but little affection. Then I
knew that the time had come to redeem my
unspoken promise, and I went to my brother
and told him what I was about to do. He
had always hated your father, with a hatred
that nothing could exceed, and on hearing that
I meant to adopt his daughter, his fury rose
to madness, and he swore that if I took you

under my care I should never enter his doors
again. When I told him my mind was made
up, he bade me begone and starve with you
—ay, starve; for all the fortune I possessed was a scanty pittance left me by my
mother—or so it seemed to one who had
never known the use of money, or the lack
of it.

"I left him and came to London, and then
my struggles began. It is difficult for a
woman to obtain a subsistence, even if she
possesses the knowledge necessary to earn
it; it is more difficult still when she knows
not how to seek it, and has no friends to
advise her; nevertheless it came to pass that
ere many months were past I was able to
fetch you to a home—a home to which you
came with passionate grief and frantic un-
willingness, for though you had lost both
your parents, yet the first real trial of your
life was your separation from Muriel, and
though I besought her to come and live with
me as well, she would not do so; she must
make her own way in the world, she said,

but would ask my leave to come and see you twice a year.

" I made her promise that she would never tell you that you were indebted to me for a home ; I thought the knowledge might fetter and gall you, so you never guessed but that your father left you in my charge, with a certain sum of money for your use and maintenance.

" And now, Mignon, the bitter gist of my story is to come, and how hard it is to me to tell you will never know . . . . it is this : At my death the paltry income that I possess passes into my brother's hands, and leaves you totally unprovided for. If I could have left you some certain yearly sum, however small, upon which you might subsist when other means failed you, I should die content, but it grieves me sorely to leave you without one creature to whom you can look for protection or help, save Prue, who loves you, and is a good woman, yet has it not in her power to do more than serve you faithfully. By patient care, I have succeeded in saving

for you the sum of a hundred pounds, which
I have paid in at the Lilytown bank, in your
real name, Gabrielle Ferrers—and that you
must almost have forgotten, since it is so
long since any one called you by it—a name
I have ever hated, since it was your mother's,
so that when, a year ago, Lu-Lu christened
you 'Mignon,' I encouraged the idea, until
at last you came to be called by that, and no
other.

"And now for the future. If I do not
return, and since I know my brother too well
to believe that he will hold out any hand of
help towards you, your best plan will be to
seek employment as governess or companion,
with Prue's help. I have already spoken to
her on the subject, and the money I have left
you will pay both her expenses and yours
until such time as you have found a shelter.
Trusting in God and your own heart, in the
integrity of your principles, in the purity of
your soul, all may yet be well with you ; and
if it should be that the love of a good man
become yours, I beseech you do not cast it

aside for any fancy, or whim, or folly, for, although you may have many lovers, there will not be many worth the taking. And I warn you against believing the passionate vehement wooer, who vows the world to be well lost for your sake, against the true and steady one, who does his duty before Heaven and his own conscience, and whose love for you is no sudden caprice born of your beauty, but a deep and steady affection that will wax deeper, not colder, as time goes by.

"You will perhaps lay down my letter here to say to yourself, 'Have I not Muriel? Can I be so friendless, when the thing I love best on earth is alive and well?' Oh! Mignon . . . . Mignon . . . . I have something to say to you. *I have received news of your sister Muriel.*"

Mignon sprang up with a low cry.

"Oh! how cruel . . . . how cruel!" she cried wildly, "never to say one word to me, and when I used to ask her every day . . . ." she broke off, suddenly conscious that she was speaking of the dead; and is there any

more shameful disloyalty on earth than to
have unkind thoughts or words for those who
can speak no syllable to reinstate themselves
in our regard ?

She seized the letter, but was so blinded
by excitement and eagerness, that the written
words danced before her eyes ; by-and-by
they steadied themselves, and she read as
follows :

" If I return safely from those lonely cities
where my restless feet bear me up and down,
backwards and forwards, as some strange yet
certain instinct to-night tells me that I shall
not return, this letter with its enclosure will
be destroyed, and of your sister you will
learn no tidings from me, until she returns to
tell you all, of her own free will ; but since it
is possible that the knowledge I possess will
be forced upon you in some unforeseen and
abrupt manner, and that the telling of the
story may come more gently from my lips
than from those of a stranger, I leave a
written account of my interview with her,
although I am bound to tell you that if you

read it, you do so in defiance of her expressed wish and command. You have your choice of two things ; you worship Muriel, and to you she is a type of perfect purity and goodness ; you could better believe evil of yourself than of her.

"Mignon, little adopted daughter, I would that you might keep your faithful, beautiful belief in Muriel always, that in your thoughts she should be ever as she is to-day, therefore I leave it in your own hands whether you destroy, unread, the letter I enclose in this, or read it, and thereby lose the purest jewel out of your life. I say I leave it in your own hands, for I am sorely perplexed between my promise to *her* and my duty to *you*. Farewell. God bless and protect you always.

"MARIE MAKEPEACE SOREL."

CHAPTER XVI.

" Anything that's mended is but patched ; virtue that transgresses is but patched with sin, and sin that amends is but patched with virtue."

IGNON walked to the window and looked out at the garden stretched below. Bumble and a favourite wife had escaped from the kitchen-garden, and were strutting about the burnt-up, stubbly bit of lawn on which reposed half a dozen bent croquet hoops, three or four battered wooden balls, and two mallets, the same being the forlorn residue of a set of croquet that had been in its prime some three years ago.

" It will rain before night," she said aloud,

and looking up at the skies, over which a lowering black cloud was slowly creeping. The air was sultry, the silence oppressive, there was but little beauty in either sky or land just then, but Mignon leant far out on the window-sill, looking abroad as though she were anxious to imprint all that she saw upon her memory. Perhaps some instinct told her that this old garden which had grown dear to her from long familiarity would never again look the same to her after to-day, that the careless happy hours of her girlhood were gone, never to return, while the cares and troubles of a woman were thickening about her path . . . . I say it may be so, for she was not conscious of thought, she simply regarded that which was before her, and understood it, noting all things, from the stray birds that flew from one tree to another, hastening to hide themselves from the coming storm, to the blood-red heart of a single rose that grew on one of the standard bushes her own hand had planted nigh upon four years ago.

A faint mutter in the distance heralded approaching mischief. Mignon withdrew from the window and went back to the table where the unopened letter lay. She took it in her hand, looked at, and laid it down again.

"Muriel," she whispered, and her voice sounded strange and sinister in the lonely, darkening room, "shall I open this letter, or destroy it, and so go back to the long and weary days of waiting, with the added misery of knowing that I might have learned somewhat of you, and did not? It holds tidings of you, and any news must be good to me after your long and cruel silence . . . . You cannot have done anything wrong, my Muriel, it is I who have been always wicked, not you! and perhaps you are expecting me—reproaching me in your heart; while I am idling here, *there* may be a message in this letter from you to me . . . . an explanation why you do not come. . . .

"Yes! I will read it, I will face the truth, whatever it may be, for nothing can break my love for you, my beloved, nothing can make you any other than my angel of goodness, and I can bear anything that brings me nearer to you, no matter how steep and thorny the path may be. . . ."

Once more she took the packet in her hand. As she broke the seal, a sudden glare of lightning half blinded her; as she drew the letter from the envelope, a clap of thunder seemed to shake the house to its foundations.

"Mignon," wrote Miss Sorel, "when a bad thing has to be told, or a blow is about to be inflicted, the only mercy that can be shown is to do it quickly; therefore I will say what I have to say in the fewest possible words.

"You know that when I brought you here, Muriel, adopting your mother's name of Brook, sought and obtained a situation as governess in the family of a Mrs. Falkner, who lived in Dublin. Twice a year she came over to spend her holidays with you. Twice a week (sometimes oftener) she wrote to you,

and for the space of over two years she failed
neither in her visits nor her correspondence.
At the end of that time all communication
with her abruptly ceased, your letters and
mine were returned to us, unopened and re-
directed by Mrs. Falkner. Upon my writing
to that lady and inquiring for your sister, I
received the intelligence that Muriel had left
her suddenly; giving no reason, leaving no
address, affording not the slightest clue by
which it was possible to ascertain her where-
abouts.

"You used to come to me and say, ' *Do
you think she is dead, ma'am?*' and my heart
grew sore for you, for I had begun to suspect
that Muriel was lost to you (let me whisper
it, Mignon ; and since I shall be dead when
you read these words, do not hate me for
what I am forced to say) by something of
which you have never heard, and cannot even
guess at . . . . something compared with
which death is kind and the grave a friend
. . . . and the name of this thing by which
she is lost to you is—*shame!*

" I say I suspected it, but I did not *know*; that was to come after.

" Do you remember the fever you had in the autumn of the year before last—how in your delirium you moaned, ' *Muriel! Muriel!*' till it almost broke one's heart to hear you ? And do you remember how, when you were beginning to recover, you used in the evening to lie in the drawing-room with Lu-Lu, or sometimes myself, for companion ? One evening I was sitting with you after dark— I in the shadow, you in the firelight with your features plainly visible—when I saw a woman's face pressed against the window-pane, peering in. She thought you alone, for her eyes never once wandered towards me ; and the intensity of her gaze, and something in the half-seen features, sent a sudden suspicion leaping through my mind. I managed to get out of the room without a sound, so that when I came behind her in the garden she was still there. I laid my hand upon her arm; she turned with a violent start and broke away from me like a mad creature, but I caught at her dress and held her fast.

" 'Muriel,' I said, ' have you come at last to see Gabrielle ?'

" ' How do you know that I am Muriel ?' she said in a strange defiant voice that staggered me.

" It was so different to the sweet voice of the girl I had spoken with only a few months before.

" She was holding a piece of her shawl over her face, we were but a few paces from the window, but it was so dark that I could no longer distinguish her features.   Nevertheless an unerring in- stinct told me that it was your sister and no other.

" I think she dropped the shawl.   I let go her dress and held her arm—a round firm arm clasped by a heavy bracelet that from the mere touch assured me she was not at all events suffering from poverty.

" ' Let me go,' she cried, struggling violently—ay, violently ; and do you remember that the distinguished quality of Muriel was her *gentleness?*

" 'Muriel,' I said, 'do you know that Gabrielle has been very ill, that the child's life has been in danger?'

" I felt her arm tremble in my grasp as though she were in an ague fit, and her voice was hoarser than before as she whispered :

" 'She is better now . . . she is recovering?'

" 'Yes,' I said, 'and strangely enough she now frets about you no longer, but seems happy in looking forward to the time when you will return to her.'

" She rocked herself to and fro in a strange dumb agony for some moments, then she said :

" 'She does not think evil of me, she does not suspect me of—*sin?*'

" My soul seemed to die within me as I heard her . . . I saw the old miserable story so plainly . . . but through it all I was most conscious of pity for *you*—you who had so loved and believed in her, who looked upon her as something above and beyond other women . . . and it seemed to me that your wreck of faith in her (when you should know all) was the most piteous feature in the whole case.

" She repeated her question almost fiercely. ' She does not suspect me of—*sin?*'

" ' She does not know the meaning of the word,' I said, ' at least in the common acceptation of the term.'

" ' God grant she never may!' cried Muriel, with fearful energy. ' Promise me, swear to me, that you never *will* tell her . . . let me be for a little longer to my angel the Muriel that she used to love . . . used to love. . . .'

" Her arms fell by her sides, she stood like a woman turned to stone, then she suddenly stooped her lips to my hands and kissed them passionately.

" ' You are a good woman,' she said, ' are you not ?'

" ' No,' I said ; ' I only try to be.'

" ' Then if you are not,' she said, ' no one

is. And a good woman always keeps her promise, does she not ?'

" ' Yes,' I said.

" ' Then promise,' she said, holding my arm tightly, 'that you will never reveal to Gabrielle that you saw me here to-night. Swear to me that you will never tell her the thoughts that I know are in your heart concerning me to-night . . . that you will utter no word to soil the purity of her mind by one whisper or hint of evil. Let her think me cruel, unnatural, heartless, but do not let her think me— wicked. You swear it ?'

" ' Upon one condition only,' I said, after a few moments of thought, ' and that is, that I leave a written account of this interview with you for Gabrielle to read in case of my death.'

" ' In case of your death ?' she cried ; 'are you ill of an incurable disease ? have you any reason to think that you are *likely* to die before long ?'

" ' No,' I said, ' I have no disease that I know of ; humanly speaking I am likely to live for a long while, but death may come unexpectedly to me, as to you, at any moment.'

" ' Do you think that you will live two years ?' she cried; 'do you think you are likely to die before that ?'

" It was a strange question asked in a strange fashion, but I perfectly understood that she wanted certain things kept from you for a certain time, and that she feared my death might interfere with her plans.

" ' I cannot tell,' I said. ' Why do you say two years ?'

" ' Because,' she said, ' by that time all will have come right, and I shall be able to face her—honest. I shall be able to look her in the face, and you, without fear or shame. You will have a better opinion of me then than you have to-night . . . if you knew what I have suffered, what I do suffer, you might find it in your heart to be sorry for me. . . .'

" She left my side, and stole to the window. I looked over her shoulder. You were sitting by the fireside working, and there was a smile upon your lips, the first I had seen there for many weeks.

"'See!' cried Muriel, 'she smiles! Gabrielle ! . . . Gabrielle !'

" There was such a passion of longing in the poor creature's voice that it made my heart ache to hear her. At last she tore herself away.

"'Think as well of me as you can,' she whispered, taking my hand in her two trembling ones ; ' you have promised that you will never tell her ?'

"' Yes,' I said, ' I have promised.'

"'God bless you,' she said, ' but above all for the friend you have been to my Gabrielle ! Do not deem me thankless of your goodness, and I dare to pray for you every day. . . .'

" And with that she kissed my hands and was gone like a shadow.

" I have only seen her once since that night; it was about three months ago. She was again looking in on you from the garden,.

but this time from the front of the house. When I reached the place where I had seen her standing, I found no sign of her. It seemed to me a curious and sad fatality that, at the very time you were at your brightest and happiest, looking forward with such unclouded hope to your reunion, I should have become possessed of the knowledge how by her own act she had severed herself from you for ever.

"Mignon, do not look for her return; better far for you that you should never see her face again . . . . lest you have to endure the inconceivable agony of contrasting the Muriel of your love and childhood with the Muriel that now lives to you; and believe me when I say that, bitter as would be her loss by death to you, it would be merciful compared with the horror of knowing her to be alive, divided from you by a gulf that she can never cross—the gulf of *sin*.

"That she will return when the two years have elapsed I hold to be too wild and improbable a story to afford us one ray of hopeful anticipation; dependent upon the capricious impulse of the man who has betrayed her, she leans but on a broken reed. . . . For so it is that when a virtuous woman forfeits the respect of the man who loves her, she makes herself but a poor dependent on his bounty, and reposes herself but by sufferance upon his protection; while he, being bound by no law to give her redress, being indeed thrown absolutely back upon the goodness of his impulses and heart as to whether or no he shall repair the wrong he has done her, is, alas! more likely to be false to his better instincts than true to them; for the tendency of a bad man is ever towards evil, and he rarely gives the lie to his past life by one deed of conspicuous virtue.

"Mignon, little adopted daughter, if my words appear heartless and cruel to you, I beseech you to believe that they are as hard to me to tell as to you to hear. . . . Comfort I cannot give you, pity I dare not offer. . . . Only believe that you are not the first, as you will not be the last, to whom God has seen fit to send so terrible a misfortune.

" MARIE MAKEPEACE SOREL."

Five minutes passed, ten minutes, fifteen. The hand of the clock went round to the half hour, but still Mignon sat still and quiet, the letter neatly refolded and placed in the envelope. A knock at the door came, and there entered Prue.

The storm had spent itself, the rain had ceased to fall, the sweet odours of flowers and refreshed green leaves floated in at the open window.

Prue advanced, about to speak, but when she saw the rigid attitude of the girl who sat in the chair, when she saw the awful change that had come over Mignon's face in the space of one hour—she stopped short, terror-struck.

" Little mistress," she cried, " don't look like that . . . . don't fret so about Miss Sorel; if you haven't got any friends or home, dear heart, you've got your poor old Prue, and together we'll make our own way in the world. . . ."

Mignon lifted her hand and beckoned to the woman. Prue came slowly nearer and nearer till she faced the girl.

" Prue," said Mignon slowly, and her voice was as the voice of a stranger, "what is *shame?*"

CHAPTER XVII.

"O limèd soul, that struggling to be free
Art more engaged !"

SOME one was watching the stars, "the angels' forget-me-nots," come out one by one in the sky overhead. O stars! that man in his short-sighted, narrow-minded wisdom calls "restless," do you not mock him, even as he speaks, with the silent majesty of your eternal peace and presence? Is it not the toiling, throbbing, suffering heart of man that is restless, not you? Century after century you look dumbly down upon millions upon millions of human beings who, in the brief and scanty hours of serenity that brighten their lives, and possessed by no immediate, passionate wish, or unfulfilled longing, lift their eyes to your supreme splendour, and, pointing at you a pigmy finger fashioned of dust, hurl at you the epithet of " restless."

You might teach us many a lesson of beauty and peace if our hearts could only be guided to read you aright. . . . You might breathe into our souls some divine image of the unutterable grandeur of the life that lies beyond this present, but we do not seek to understand you, or fathom the mystery of your meaning. . . . We just glance up at you for a few seconds with careless, aweless regard, as though you were pretty toys hung out for our passing wonder and amusement, then turn our eyes downwards to the coarse and garish lights that guide our footsteps, and death overtakes us while we are still groping to and fro, seeking for the jewel of wisdom in the mud that hampers our feet; having learned not one lesson from those simple yet mighty teachers overhead, nor attained to either knowledge, understanding, or greatness.

Some one was thinking, as so many other souls have thought in their misery (and most of them I think in their youth, when trouble seemed to them a less natural thing than happiness ; whereas to the older wayfarers, happiness is accepted as something strange and precious, theirs by no right of their own, but a gift sent straight from Heaven), " It will be all the same a hundred years hence."

This cry, that proceeds from such different natures, under such widely different circumstances, must surely take its root in some process of reasoning that is gone through alike by all suffering human nature .... or perhaps it is the outcome of a sudden lightning conviction of the utter impotence and wasteful-ness of sorrow, and our intense weariness of life causes us to look forward to the annihila-tion of it, and all it knows and comprehends, with a certain sense of relief.   But although the mere utterance of the old, old thought carries with it a dull comfort of its own, reality steps quickly in and pricks us with the thought that the hundred years are not over yet, that the *meanwhile* alone is our life and must be gathered up and borne as a burthen, no matter

how the flagging limbs fail us, no matter that
we see no end or turning to the dark and
lonely road along which our journey lies, nor
that there is not one breast to which we bear a
claim upon which to lay the burning brow for
one precious purchase-hour of peace . . . .

" Nothing cares," thought the girl as she
lifted her heavy eyes—eyes that had shed no
tears throughout these seven long days—to
the crescent-shaped moon, that

> " Put forth a little diamond peak,
> No bigger than an unobservèd star,
> Or tiny point of fairy scimitar.
> Bright signal that she only stooped to tie,
> Her silver sandals ere deliciously
> She bowed into the heavens her timid head."

A night-bird whirled swiftly past . . . out
of the soft twilight a night-wind came sighing
and whispering, toying with the few precious
flowers brought by Prue, that

> " Poured out their soul in odours,
> That were their prayers and confessions ;"

and the peace and stillness of the soft summer night warred against the girl's passionate heart, and she cried out dumbly against the heartlessness of nature, as though she expected the stars to step down and comfort her, the bird to pause in his flight to whisper consolation, the very foundations of all things to be upheaved because she was so tossed upon the waves of shame and agony . . . . but there came no voice out of the night, no sign out of the silence, and so in her confused longing after something that she could not compass, she had said in her bitterness of spirit, " Nothing cares." Who has not felt, at some period or other of his existence, that Nature is a cruel and unsympathising mother to the children who love her best ?

Go to her when you are happy and contented, and she will seem to rejoice and make merry with you. . . . Every one of her quivering lights and delicate tints will be a message from her heart to yours, that she knows your secret, and exults in your gladness. . . . The music of her waterfalls will

be as the sound of her voice, the breath of
her flowers as the words of her lips, the sunlight upon her purple hills will be as a smile
that is smiled for you, and you alone, and
your heart will borrow a quicker throb and
beat at feeling how perfectly it is in unison
with hers . . . . but go to her when you are
sad and lonely, when the only creature from
whom you could brook the receiving of pity
is far away, and she will heed you not . . . .
nor shed one tear over your sorrow, nor
silence one song of her countless birds, nor
quench one of her magic lights . . . . nay, if
you die, she will wear her fairest robe, her
brightest smile, and at the very moment of
your departure, she will produce some magical
effect of sunlit leaf and landscape that you
should, on beholding it in your moments of
felicity, have deemed to be a special and
loving token of her harmony with your
soul. . . . And yet the great nurse-mother
has a heart, and a very human one, for while
she still continues to smile for they of her
children who are light of heart, she receives

her dead and sorrowful ones tenderly into her bosom. . . . Over their heads she sows her delicate flowers and kindly grasses, and out of the hum of the bees, the chorus of her silver-throated choir of birds, the very rustle of her silken leaves, nay, the very footfall of her shy and beautiful animal creation, she weaves one exquisite, never-failing requiem to sing over them, remembering, when all human things, ay, even they that have loved them most tenderly, have utterly forgotten!

"Nothing cares." But little farther on its way of research groped the confused and childish intelligence of the lonely little creature who sat, very still and drooping, in the old wooden chair.

There was something strangely pathetic in its absolute quietude, for in Mignon's short life it had ever been her nature to cry out sharply under pain of body or mind; but the bitterness of an adversity that was in itself irreversible, and set far beyond the merciful chance of either hope or fear, had absolutely stunned her with its violence, leaving her with no more than a crushed and helpless feeling of accomplished misery.

In the days of her keenest longing after Muriel, she had owned one precious possession, of which no man had power to rob her, that had been the tide upon which floated, fair and stately, the argosy of her hopes, laden with the golden store of love and happiness, liable to no storms from without, no treachery from within, as are the brave ships that sail upon the dangerous shifting floods of reality. . . . Now the future had stepped backwards and become the present, and she saw it, this dream-joy of her fancy, as the hollow, pitiful mockery that it was, devoid of substance, use, or fulfilment, how its boards were rotten, its yards manned by the dead, its sails but skeleton hands that waved idly in the wind, the ghastly wraith of that cursed and cruel "might have been" that draws all the sweetness and pith from out of human lives to cast it down as water upon the earth.

To Mignon all things began and ended in
the present—the present, that her immature
powers of suffering did not give the strength
and resolution to meet . . . . she was as
one who is suddenly deprived of the crutch
upon which she has confidingly leaned in
her troublous path, and knows not how to
take one single step forward without its
support.

She did not even dimly guess how Time,
the Restorer, heals all wounds . . . . even if
she had known it, would not her soul have
rebelled against the hurt that she had received, unconsciously asking what healed
wound could ever compare with the unflawed
wholeness that was hers ere the knife was
lifted and the blow fell ? What restoration
can ever compare with the dauntless confidence of untried and unbroken health ?
The stain may be cleansed away, but the
traces of the process remain . . . . the gaping
wound may close, but the scar remains for
ever . . . . we can lay our fingers upon it at
any moment, and say to our hearts, " It is

here " . . . . and we feel it throb and burn for many a year after others deem it wholly healed and forgotten; we remember, as no other can, what we were in the days before we tasted of the fruit of the tree of knowledge . . . . we know what we now are . . . . not to mortals is it given to eat of the tree of knowledge either in the shape of sin or sorrow, and henceforward be as though our shrinking lips had never touched it.

The night drew in, the countless hosts of the great army of living lights overhead had ceased to gather, and now filled the appointed places set by Him of whom it has been written, "He calleth them all by their names " . . . . but the girl still sat without stir or movement, trying painfully to think, yet hearing only a dumb cry from all creation, the skies, the earth, the wind, of *Muriel! Muriel!* And so it was that her ears were deaf to the sound of footsteps that came slowly along the gravel walk, nor did she lift her eyes when they approached nearer,

nearer, and at length came to a full stop before her.

There was enough light in the sky for the new-comer to make out the outline of a fair, drooped head, and of two little slim hands, folded stiffly on a plain black gown.

"Gabrielle Ferrers !"

It was a man's voice that spoke, harsh and distinct, each word falling sharply upon the silence with startling effect.

She raised her head slowly, like a dull or chidden child, with whom obedience, however painful, is an instinct.

"Stand up !" he said.

She rose, in a strange mechanical fashion, and quietly, with no sense of wonder or of fear, discovered in the half-light the unforgotten face of Silas Sorel.

He put out his hand and touched a fold of her black dress. "You wear this for your benefactress ?" he said.

She bowed her head in silence. The sources of speech, as those of thought, seemed, for the time being, to be dried up.

"You have reason to regret her," he said coldly, "for she was the only friend you possessed in the world. There are men and women altogether independent of friendship and extraneous support, who find their best and safest allies in themselves, and possess the power to carve out their own lives boldly and well; but you are not one of these women; your father was not one of these men; you are all unstable; and as a sapless tree or a drought-stricken land, shall you wither away, root and branch, and your place shall know you no more."

The even voice, broken neither by anger nor passion, uttered these words with the solemnity of a curse, and Mignon, listening to him with patient care, and no shadow of either fear or resentment, unconsciously committed them to memory, knowing not that in an unknown day of the future they would recur to her mind with all the force and significance of a prophecy.

"Facile as sand, weak as water, with headstrong hearts and feeble wills, you are all bound to fulfil your destinies. Already, from afar off, I have watched the working out of those of your father and sister, and yours will in no sense be behind the others, or I have not read that true Ferrers face of yours aright."

He paused. The scorn that for one moment thrust aside her pall of wretchedness, and flashed from her eyes, might surely have wakened in him some dormant spark of manliness, had he not been sexless through his madness. . . . A spirit of revengeful hatred, immoderately nourished and exalted into godship, has the effect of divesting both man and woman of every human attribute where the object of its loathing is concerned, making of them but blind instruments of a cowardly and degrading passion.

" Such being the case," Mr. Sorel went on, " the death of my sister is in every way disastrous to you. Had she lived, your home with her would have been secured until some man, mad and senseless enough to be caught by your pretty wax-doll face, spoilt his life by marrying you ; but as it is you are deprived of your home, you have not a single friend, and you will have to earn your bread before you eat it. The world in general is apt to be cold to those who look to it for subsistence—cold, yet in some respects too kind for the safety of a young and friendless woman."

His latter words fell unheeded on Mignon's ears . . . . with her lately acquired terrible knowledge of sin fresh upon her, she yet did not understand him, so that the insult of his insinuation, the degradation of his speech, simply recoiled upon himself, and he knew it. His hatred and bitterness of heart rose higher as he saw how powerless he was to move her . . . . he knew nothing of the history of her griefs, he believed her silence and immobility to be but an insolent and audacious phase of the Ferrers' haughtiness and pride of bearing, and his slow pulses quickened with anger as he cried :

"Do you know what she was to me, this dead woman, who was the sweetheart of your father, the friend of his child, the gentle schoolmistress to an army of turbulent girls that her weak hand had scarcely power to control? She was my very life itself. Any pretty fool would have suited your father just as well as she did; any commonplace woman could have done as much for you as she has done; but nothing would serve but that my own joy upon earth should be sacrificed at the altar of you and yours. . . . . A harsh, unloved man, I was a yet more cursed and unhappy child; my very mother could not endure my evil humours, my father spurned me from his path; only one creature bore with me, understood me, loved me . . . . ay! in spite of all my hatefulness *loved* me, and that was the dead sister upon whom I looked my last four days ago, and who would be with me now but for you and yours . . . . you and yours. . . . . It was no bodily illness that killed my poor girl, it was a broken heart—do you hear me? A broken heart, and your father was the man that broke it. . . . . He had all the world to choose from,

yet he must needs come and steal from me
my one ewe lamb. I endured to see her
drift away from me, endured to see the
passionate love of a week set aside the deep
and steady attachment of years, for I loved
her too well not to be able to endure my own
loss if it should result in her happiness, only
it was not so . . . . the treasure that he had
grasped with such eager avaricious hands, ere
long fell from them, and on the day that she
should have become his wife, her heart broke
instead, and I, O God! in my madness was
as Cain, and would have followed and killed
him, had she not wrung from me a promise
that I would never lay hand upon him. . . . . ..
It was not his fault, she said—not his fault!
O Heavens! And thus for many years we
dwelt together, but a gulf yawned between
us, the old days never came back, she was no
longer my sister, but *his* sweetheart. . . . .
She came to me one day and told me that he
was dead. I rejoiced, thinking 'now that he
is gone her heart will turn back to me.' And
even as he had been to her living, so was he

to her dead.   Not long afterwards she came
to me again, and said that he had left a child
in her care, and that she was resolved upon
accepting the trust.   I bade her choose
between us, and she chose — you.   The
patient love of a lifetime to weigh not a
feather against the dying wish of the man
who had duped her!   Judge then whether or
no I have reason to hate you, ay, even more
than I hated your father. . . . Judge when
from time to time I saw her, growing paler
and paler, flagging more and more under the
burden your selfish father imposed upon her,
whether I did not transfer my hatred from
your father, dead, to his daughter, living;
judge whether I am likely to raise my hand
to save you from the miserable future that
awaits you, for even as your ill-starred father
perished, even as your sister is living in
shame, so shall the horror of your future in
no way fall behind that of the others, and I
shall live to see it, ay! and behold you perish
even as the Book has written that all the
seed of the unrighteous shall perish. . . . ."

He lifted his hand in solemn warning, his voice was terrible in its monotony, he was in truth a fanatic, whose brain had been partially overturned by intense brooding on the subject of his sister's wrongs and his own, and there was the glare of covert madness in his eyes as he peered through the half-light into the girl's face. She, recoiling at those pale and frightful features, fell back before him, and he, still advancing, was face to face with her as she stood upright against the wall, whereat, her courage suddenly failing her, and the power of speech returning, she suddenly shrieked out " ADAM !"

CHAPTER XVIII.

"Friend! is there any such foolish thing in the world?"

THE cry had preceded the thought by about a second, instinct directed it, for it was the result of no conscious volition of her own.

A breathless silence followed, which lasted some ten seconds. Then a man dropped noiselessly from the wall almost at their feet.

"You called me?" he said, intensely relieved at finding nothing more terrible going forward than Mignon in apparently close conversation with a middle-aged and extremely ill-favoured gentleman; for the cry had been such as one might utter in the extremity of fear or anguish, and had pierced his ear with a sudden and disastrous foreboding of evil.

"An assignation, I presume," said Silas Sorel, withdrawing a few steps from the pair; "you are beginning early, Gabrielle Ferrers."

The tone of the man who spoke, conveyed a deliberate insult to the girl, none to Adam, and the latter perfectly understood him.

"An assignation," he said calmly, "is a thing that requires a previous agreement between two persons, and that such is not the case this evening, is proved by the fact that I am only here in obedience to Miss Ferrers' summons"

"Take care, take care," said Mr. Sorel, addressing Mignon, and disregarding Adam utterly, "that you do not follow the example of the girl that you call Muriel!"

"Peace!" cried Mignon, stepping forward, the *fierté* of her voice and attitude amazing the one man as thoroughly as the other; "do not dare to take her name between your foul and lying lips   Revile the dead if you will; they are beyond the reach of your curses as

of your hatred for ever, and you can wreak
no pitiful revenge upon them ; revile the
living that are face to face with you, but do
not dare to traduce one who is not here to
speak for herself !"

She turned back to Adam, as though he
were her friend and refuge, and indeed she
had altogether forgotten her cause for anger
against him, instinct guided her to him, and
she went. . . . . The Ithuriel spear of sorrow
had turned all lesser things into shadows at a
touch, and a passionate throb of exultation
ran through Adam's bewilderment that it
should be so, that the wild and improbable
dreams of an hour ago should in a breath have
leaped to golden fruition, that he was actually
in her presence, called thither by her voice,
looked to by her for help and protection,
nay, more, that he dared to hold one of her
little trembling hands securely in his
own.

" Who is this man ?" he said to her ; " and
by what right does he come here to thus
insult you ?"

"He is my enemy," said Mignon, "and he has no authority over me."

"This young lady, sir," said Silas, extending his hand towards her, and for the first time addressing Adam, "enjoys the proud position of owning not one soul upon earth who has the smallest authority over her; but as a slight drawback to her enviable position, she is an absolute pauper, without a shilling or a friend in the world, and not a home open to her save that which is furnished by a sister's shame."

"You lie!" cried Adam, dropping Mignon's hand and striding forward. "She has a friend, and he is—*here!*"

He struck his breast with a vehement gesture, the longing strong upon him to seize the man before him and inflict upon him the chastisement he so richly deserved.

"And so you are her friend?" said Silas with a sneer, and again the deliberate insult his tone conveyed made the blood boil in Adam's veins. "Did I not tell you, girl, that you would find the world, cold as it usually is, in some respects too kind to you? And we all understand what kind of friendship subsists between a young lady who is on such excellent terms of clandestine intimacy with a young man that a call will at any moment bring him to her side!"

" Sir!" cried Adam, almost beside himself with fury, " do not presume too greatly upon your grey hairs, although the man who can thus shelter himself behind them is so vile a coward that he deserves to take a coward's punishment. And as to your calumnies, I hurl them back in your teeth."

" Bah!" said Silas scornfully; " you use long words, but ask her if what I have said is not true, every word of it."

Mignon's head had sunk upon her breast; a burning shame was upon her; she could not have put her hand in Adam's now if her life had depended upon it, but he took it in his own and—

" Sir," he said, " I think you must hate this young lady very much, although I cannot conceive it possible that she has ever harmed you."

"I hate her," said Silas, slowly; "she and all her stock. The men are all fickle, the women are all light; there is not one sound fruit upon the tree; have naught to do with them if you desire any peace of mind, or covet an unstained life; better far that you should die by your own hand than place your honour in the hands of a Ferrers."

In the days to come these words were to ring in Adam's ears and be to him as letters of fire in the darkness, as letters of ink in the sunshine . . . although they were now but as the angry, futile ravings of an embittered, half-maddened man.

"Have you anything more to say?" said Adam quietly; "if not, I charge you begone, ere I force you from the gentle presence that you have so outraged by your wicked, lying words."

"Before you bid your elders and betters begone, young man," said Silas, "you had better be quite sure of whose premises you are standing upon.   Now, as it happens, this garden is mine, whereas you committed a trespass by entering it by way of the wall ; therefore it is for me to command your departure, scarcely for you to command mine."

"But," said Adam, looking down at the girl who stood beside him, "is not Miss Sorel——"

"Miss Sorel is dead," said Silas fiercely ; "and as her property reverts to me, this garden is mine.   Yonder house and all that it contains is mine.   You will leave it," he said to Mignon, "by the day after to-morrow at sundown ; you will take with you that beggarly woman who has for you so great an affection ; and you will leave not one trace of your sojourn there, or one indication that will serve to remind me of your existence, nor will you dare to again cross the threshold of the house that has sheltered you for so long. Henceforth your place is out in the world."

"Oh ! have mercy !" cried Mignon, falling on her knees ; "and do not drive me away before she has come back . . . . she would think I was dead, or had forgotten her, and she would go wandering about looking for me . . . . and we should never find each other . . . . let me starve, live in the meanest corner of it, or in this old garden, do humblest service for you ; but oh ! do not send me away !"

A mist swept across Adam's eyes ; a lump in his throat half-strangled him, as he stooped over that little kneeling figure, and raised it in his arms.

" No," said Silas ; " you shall not live here. If she returns (and it's not likely) I will bid her follow you ; you will probably wander about half your lives looking for each other, and that will be a worse punishment than if you found her now, although she is what she is."

A low cry of agony broke from the girl's lips . . . . his wicked words passed her by ; she was conscious of but one thought, that she was to be banished from the place to which Muriel would so certainly, whether in triumph or degradation, sooner or later return.

"Mignon," said Adam, " if it be true that you are so lonely, having neither father nor mother, nor any friend at hand to take care of you, will you take *me* for your friend, lover, and husband ? Will you come tc such a home as I can give you, where we will together wait for Muriel's return ?"

He felt a quiver pass through her, as though she were violently surprised and startled, but she answered him never a word. How the brave, true heart beat, as he looked across at Silas, who had retreated a step and seemed struck with a bitter and angry dismay.

" You would *marry* her ?" he cried.

" Ay !" said Adam, " if she will take me ; if she will stoop to lay her little hand in mine, all unworthy as I am, and give me the right to cherish and protect her always ; so much I would do for her, so help me God !"

" You would take her !" cried Silas, " with the knowledge lying at your heart like a viper that all the Ferrers are bad—bad ; that sooner or later the black drop will come out in yonder girl; that sooner or later—for they are all false—she will betray you?"

"I would take her," said Adam, never loosening his hold upon the girl's drooping, quiet figure, "with all her childish faults and imperfections, with her beautiful youth, her unsoiled freshness and innocent heart, and deem her the most precious and gentle gift that ever came to the heart of man . . . . I would commit my honour to her keeping, and lay my future in her hands without one doubt as to their safety, or one fear of her disloyalty; if she were able to find within her heart one little word of kindness for a poor fellow who loves, yet is not half worthy of her."

"You love me?" exclaimed Mignon.

"I have loved you for a long while."

This new puzzle for the moment distracted her attention from other things; she stood quite still, conscious, for the first time that night, of thought. Impulse and instinct had hitherto guided all her words and actions.

The two men waited, breathless, for a reply. One at least would have forecast her

future with a certain amount of truth had that
answer been in the negative.

" You would help me to find her ?" she
said, pursuing a certain train of thought, and
looking earnestly into Adam's half-seen face.

" I would."

" And let me live close by here with Prue,
so that we might take it in turn to watch by
the gates, in case *she* came ?"

" Yes, you should live close by."

She put her hand to her head.

" Wait a moment," she said, " I have got
a hundred pounds, my very own ; would it
buy a roof to shelter Prue and me, and feed
and clothe us for some time, perhaps only
until the autumn comes, perhaps a great deal
longer ?"

" It would not last a great while."

She fell to thinking again ; then said :

" And if she did not come here, if it were
necessary, you would with me search the
world through from end to end until we had
found her ?"

He hesitated a moment . . . " Yes," he said.

She turned without a word and put both her hands into his. Adam held her fast, but did not speak. So they faced the enemy, young, ever brave, and handsome . . . . so he beheld them afterwards defying him. Even so in the future one of them at least remembered that cruel wicked face, and the mirthless smile that curled his thin and bloodless lips as he stood, his arms folded, looking at them.

" I wish you joy of her," he said coldly. " When we meet again, it will be a matter of the profoundest amazement to me if I discover that this young lady still retains the place in your esteem that she at this moment occupies. Miss Ferrers—sir—I have the honour to wish you a very good-evening."

CHAPTER XIX.

" Half happy by comparison of bliss, is miserable."

S the echo of his footsteps died away, Adam looked down thoughtfully into that pale young face. It took a faint warmth beneath his gaze, for she was ashamed . . . in a moment's space he had been transformed from her friend and champion to a scarcely known lover, whose presence filled her with uneasiness . . . . the former had been something to hold fast by and value, the latter oppressed her with a dull sense of discomfort and strangeness.

He was instantly conscious of the change in her, but did not let her go.

" Mignon," he said, " after all is your

answer '*No*'?" But, as he looked, he found himself no longer seeking the answer to his question, but recognising, with a sense of shock and dismay, the change that had come over her face during these past ten days, and not possessing the key of the puzzle beyond the fact of Miss Sorel's death (for that other black misfortune as shadowed forth in Mr. Sorel's speech he had rejected as a wilful and malevolent lie), he was at a loss to comprehend it.

" I am tired," she said slowly. Then, when she was seated, he knelt down by her side, on the very spot, as it suddenly occurred to him, where Rideout had knelt, a fortnight ago that very day.

The girl did not speak . . . . a wheel seemed to be going round and round in her head . . . . the waters of affliction, held back for a brief period by the strange events of the past hour, were rushing back upon her with resistless fury, and again, her soul and heart and body were one yearning bitter cry of "Muriel" . . . . " Muriel " . . . . while her sole consciousness was one of intolerable shame and misery. Presently she looked up, and seeing Adam's face close to her, a ray of curiosity flashed across the confused horror of her own.

" How long ago was it," she said slowly, " that I called you a liar, and a thief, and a spy ?"

" A long while ago," he said gently; " do not think about it."

" And after calling you those names," she went on more slowly still, " you offer me a home and . . . . your love.   For you said you loved me ?"

" Yes."

" No, you do not," she said in the same stiff, careful way; " you only pity me. . . . . How can you love a person who said such things to you ?   You only said so out of kindness, and to show that bad old man I had one friend."

" Mignon," he said, " I have been your faithful lover longer than you think, even before I came over the wall and weeded your garden. . . . . I have watched you growing up for these past two years, for I said to myself, ' When she is old enough I will go to Miss Sorel and ask her openly for leave to try and win her for my little sweet-heart.' "

" And that was why you came over the garden-wall ?" she said.

" No ; I had not meant to approach you in any clandestine manner, but a foolish impulse prompted me . . . . at that time of the morning I never dreamt of your coming out ; but you came, and then——" He paused, but she seemed to have relapsed into apathy, and did not speak.

" At first you believed me to be the man who had written you the love-letter, then, before I had in any way recovered from the confusion into which I was thrown by your sudden appearance (for remember that I loved you, and was now for the first time in your presence), you asked me whom I might be ? In the moment that I hesitated, I saw your eyes fall upon my shirt-sleeves, an inspiration flashed through my mind, and almost before the thought had formed itself, my lips had uttered the *sobriquet* given me by my sister Flora, ' Adam, the gardener.' "

" She calls you that ?"

" The term is applied contemptuously," he said. " All my life long I have been fond of working in my garden, and she is pleased to marvel at the lowness of my tastes."

" Then it was not quite a lie," said the girl, sighing, " but you should not have come again . . . . you would not have acted dishonestly then. . . ."

" No," he said, " I should not have come again, but the temptation was too great to be resisted . . . . to look, not furtively, but openly, at your face, to hear your voice, to have you addressing me, and to watch you, yourself so utterly unconscious, it was not in human nature to cast this delight away, and so I followed you, in some clothes borrowed for the purpose, to Mme. Tussaud's, and afterwards I came over and weeded your gravel-walks."

" But why did you steal the letter ?" she

said, still trying, through all her giddy sense of confusion and misfortune, to follow out a line of special thought.

"Because, at that time "—he laid a certain stress upon the last three words that Mignon did not observe—" I would rather have seen the girl I loved in her coffin, than receiving or replying to a letter from the man whom you knew as Philip Rideout, and "—his voice grew lower—" it maddened me to think that to this man, who was in no sense fit to approach you, should be written your first love-letter. . . . ."

"Then you *were* listening," cried Mignon, shrinking from him, "you watched me write it from the other side of the wall ?"

"Yes," said Adam slowly, "I listened to you. . . . . I could not love you as I do to-night if I did not know every thought of your innocent heart . . . . if I were not so sure that your face is but the reflection of your mind, if I had not assured myself with my own ears that I had not erred in placing all the hopes of my life upon you. Neverthe-

less " (he sighed, sharply and bitterly), " it
was a fatal mistake, Mignon."

He paused for some seconds, then went on
again.

"Mignon," he said, "there is one thing that I
have to tell you—and perhaps when it is told
you will bid me go away from you, for it may
be that to *him* you have given your first fancy,
and when you become aware "—he paused.

" It is this," he said firmly : " the man you
know as Mr. Rideout is free to woo you
honestly to be his wife."

" Then that too . . . . was another lie ?" she
said almost in a whisper.

O Mignon ! . . . . Mignon, how could
you . . . . he turned aside, asking himself
how he was to expect the honour and duty of
a wife from one who doubted the truth of
every syllable he spoke ?

A bad beginning ! A bad beginning !

" No," he said, " it was true."

" But you said he was married ?"

" He was—at that time."

" Then is his wife dead ?"

" No—not dead."

How could he tell this girl the whole shameful story? His lips refused to utter it . . . . it was curious that the two utterly dissimilar men, who were fated to be the joy and misery of Mignon's life, were equally careful over the purity of her mind, and that both were so passionately desirous of keeping from her the knowledge of evil.

She remained so still, that Adam said, " Are you thinking, Mignon, that you would have been happier with him ? That if I had not scared you by a warning, you would have chosen him—not me ?"

" No," she said at last, " but I was thinking . . . . that perhaps (if you are quite sure that he is free) I might have married *him* and saved you the trouble . . . . for I do not think he would have *minded* marrying me, he seemed so very sure and certain that he *did* want to marry me, and was so angry when I said ' No ' . . . . whereas you only asked me out of kindness, because you heard that wicked man say I had no friends ; and

indeed it was a generous and noble thing of
you to do, but I do not wish to take *advantage* of it, because I like you better than I
do him, though I dare say he would help
me to find *her* as well as you could, and
I think he would be really *grateful* to me if
I said ' Yes.' . . . ."

" But if you like me best," he said, clinging resolutely to the only crumb of comfort
that her speech contained, " why should you
marry him, for I love you too ?"

" But he will be so angry," said Mignon
wearily, her interest beginning to flag ; " he
said if I dared to marry any one else he
would follow me through the world, but he
would find me at last, and really I think he
is quite determined enough to do it."

" I shall know how to protect my own,"
said Adam gravely ; " and when did he say
he should return, Mignon ?"

" He said that I was to look for him
any hour after the fourteenth day had
passed."

" And the fortnight is up to-day," said

Adam ; "he may be here to-morrow—to-night even !"

The girl's head had drooped again, she did not even hear him, her soul had gone back to Muriel again.

Adam was thinking deeply. " I will not hasten things by one hour on his account," he said to himself, " but if he should come, it will be a bad business—bad."

"Adam," said Mignon almost in a whisper, " you heard what he said—that wicked man, about *her* ?"

" Yes."

" It is true," she whispered back again, " or so they say. . . ."

He did not immediately speak ; this reve-lation of her family life was terrible to him . . . . up to this time he had not believed the words of Silas Sorel, although he knew some strange mystery hung about the fate of Mignon's sister. . . . Like all men, he wished the surroundings of the woman he loved to be absolutely unassailable, and was not proof against the world's decree that, whereas the

evil doings of the male members of a family
may disgrace and bring the same into dis-
repute, yet will no real stigma attach itself to
its women, until one of the sisterhood shall
stoop to sin, and thereby for ever sully those
other innocent creatures who are guiltless
of aught save their fatal relationship to her.

"They say it is true . . . ." went on
Mignon piteously, " and they ought to know
better than I ; but how could she be wicked,
and she said she would come back at the end
of two years honest ? . . . ."

And then Adam felt, with a sharp sudden
pang of grief, that all his care for her had
been in vain . . . . that her mind was no
longer a page upon which had been written
no word of sin, or harmful meaning.

" When my poor love comes back to me,"
ran on the girl's soft voice, " as she will come
to me some night or day, you will not by
word or look show her that she is unwelcome,
or drive her away ?"

" I will not drive her away," he said
slowly, but in his heart he was praying

that she might never come back to reflect her own shame upon her sinless little sister.

"The only creature that I love in the whole world," she said, below her breath, "the heart of my heart, the life of my life. . . . ."

He heard her, but was in no whit dismayed. How could he expect her to love him yet ? While he had been learning her disposition, studying her face, he had been a perfect stranger to her, and he was not one to value hasty love . . . . he knew that a fancy may be born at first sight, but that love grows, even as the appetite by what it feeds upon, and he had infinite hopes of the future. . . . .

"We will not draw down the blinds at night," she said dreamily, "lest she should come and look in and we should not see her, but some night, *some* night, I shall see her beautiful pale face against the glass, as Miss Sorel did, and then I shall run out and bring her in . . . . at home at last. . . ."

He shivered. "Mignon," he said presently, "did you hear what Mr. Sorel said ? That yonder house was his and all within it, and that you must go away from it on the day after to-morrow ?"

"I had forgotten," she said, putting her hand to the brow that ached so terribly ; "but he cannot prevent me from sitting at his gates ; a beggar has a right to do that— *any one.*"

"I have a plan in my head," he said soothingly, "by which it is possible we may regain possession of the house, but to carry it out we must be very quiet and cautious, or he will discover it all, and thwart us—in short, Mignon, we must go away."

"*Go away ?*" she repeated blankly ; "but indeed I cannot—I cannot—it is quite impossible !"

"But, Mignon, you must," said Adam firmly, "unless you mean to lose all chance of living here, and you do not wish to do that ?"

"How long should we be away ?" said

Mignon anxiously; " three days—a week—
a fortnight ?"

" I cannot tell," he said; " it will depend
upon the length of time certain matters take
to arrange."

" And the sooner I go away, the sooner I
shall come back — is it so?" she asked
feverishly.

" Yes."

" Then let us go to-morrow morning," she
cried; " it will not take me an hour to pack
up, and——"

" But, Mignon," said the young man, half-
laughing, half-hesitating, " we must be married first; you know !"

" I had forgotten all about that," she said,
suddenly sobered; " but it doesn't take very
long—to get married, does it ?"

" No."

" I don't see why we should be married at
all," she said wistfully; " why can't you be
kind to me always and look after me ? for I
have got a lot of money—oh, a great deal, that
I dare say would last me till Muriel comes

back, and then we could go away and make
some more together—"

"Mignon," he said gently, "I am not
your brother, so I could not look after you
and take care of you as if I were one,
and I do not think you know how hard a
young girl like you would find the world ; and
you promised me, Mignon . . . ."

"If you are quite sure," said the girl,
"that you do not *mind* marrying me very
much, and that you will not some day be
sorry for having done so kind a thing, why,
then, I will marry you to-morrow—next day
—whenever you please, only *make haste* and
bring me back again !"

That imploring voice . . . he turned aside
from it and groaned, for how could he ask
her to try and understand marriage ? "To
marry" was to her to sit in that garden, to
watch at yon gates, to search the world
through for her lost sister, but of what a
wife was, she had about as much comprehen-
sion as a baby . . . .

"Then we will be married the day after to-morrow," he said, and put his arms round her and gently drew the weary head down to his shoulder.

But as he stroked the folds of the sunny hair that flooded his breast with sunshine, he said to himself, " It has all been too quick . . . . too quick . . . . could I but have had time, she might have learned to love me . . . and were it not for Philip La Mert, I would wait; but lest he snatch my prize from me, I must go on with it; only it is a pity—a pity —more, it is not fair to her, and it is hard to me . . . ."

A dusky shadow stepped out of the gloom, and looked down with amazement upon the young man supporting the girl, who was too worn out with misery, excitement, and pain to reject that kindly aid . . . .

"Prue," said Adam, touching a fold of Mignon's black dress, " will you get ready a plain white gown for your mistress ? for she is going to marry me the day after to-morrow."

CHAPTER XX.

" Had I your tongue and eyes I'd use them so
That heaven's vault should crack.
O !   She is gone for ever !"

 SLIM young figure in a white
gown, standing before a looking-
glass, fastening a white rose against
a soft, round throat . . . . a woman standing
by, divided between smiles and weeping . . .
a young man pacing a garden with rapid, unfaltering footsteps, and glancing from time to
time at the watch he holds in his hand . . . .
a weary haggard lover hasting as fast as
horse's feet will carry him to the longed-for
consummation of his dearest hopes, his most
ardent desires, while his eager imagination
outspeeds his tarrying body, and pictures to

him the form, the face, the very robe even of
the girl whom we saw but now looking in her
mirror .... an elderly clergyman walking
slowly up the narrow path that leads to the
vestry door, marvelling a little at the short
notice he has received of the marriage he is
about to celebrate .... a pew-opener, de-
ciding that for folks who are going to be
married without friends, carriages, brides-
maids, or anything whatever that befits the
occasion, she need make no attempt at their
reception beyond setting the church-door half
open, and dusting the altar steps . . . These
are the pieces that will by-and-by fit into the
morning's puzzle, and fall into their places one
by one, making the picture that is painted
upon them fair and complete.

Only one actor in the little drama (to drop
one metaphor and adopt another) cannot fail
but arrive too late .... though he were
keenly alive to the danger that threatened
him, he could not but be too late ....
for fear and apprehension could beckon
him forward no more irresistibly than does

love with its smiling, wooing, as yet untasted lips of welcome !

*   *   *   *   *

The bride, with neither smile, nor blush, nor tear, has made her vows, and her husband has kissed her upon the mouth, for the first time. The waiting-woman no longer hovers between joy and sorrow, her face is as bright as the sunlight that falls on the red and black tiles at her feet. The clergyman has shut his book, and is wondering, half sadly, quite kindly, how it comes that this young girl has no friend to stand beside her, or relation to forbid her marrying so young . . . . for to him it seems almost a profanation of the sacredness of childhood . . . . and his glance turns from the girl to rest reproachfully upon Adam. And the man who is now nearing his destination, feels his pulses bound, his heart stand still in the expectation of the vision and greeting that he so fondly believes to await him . . . .

*   *   *   *   *

They are out of the church; they have signed their names in the big register, Mignon has signed her Christian name without even knowing what may be the one for which she has exchanged it. Then she has said " good morning " to the clergyman, just as though she were used to being married every morning of her life, and put her hand in Adam's and come away, quite simply and gladly, with her head full of the thought that the sooner she shall go away the sooner she will return .... and so they go along the quiet roads together to Rosemary, where the travelling-carriage waits, ready packed and loaded, and with nothing for them to do but just jump in, take their seats, and set off upon their travels. For the rest, they had breakfasted two hours ago, and within doors there was not a soul to bid them good-bye and good luck, or send a slipper and a shower of rice flying after their chariot wheels.

At the gate Mignon drew her hand away. " I am going to say good-bye to my garden," she said, and he, understanding her humour, went into the house to speak with Prue, and she passed on her way alone.

She sat down on the old wooden chair and looked around her. Everything looked the same, yet not the same . . . . the world and all things within it had changed to her in more ways than one since the time when she rode in her wheelbarrow with such grand content, and was as happy as the days were long . . . . and now she was riding away, in a real coach, taking with her a heavier heart than she had ever dreamed of then . . . .

The sound of the familiar bang of the garden-door made her look up, thinking that it was Adam come to fetch her. In the act of rising, she involuntarily sat down again, as she recognised in the new-comer, not Adam, but Philip Rideout. Worn by fasting, excitement, and want of rest, haggard with the consuming flame of gnawing remorse, and uncontrollable passion, his dark face startled her with its wild beauty, as, hastily traversing the few steps that lay between them, and

kneeling down by her side, he clasped his arms
about her waist, and—

" Kiss me, Mignon !" he cried, " for I come
back to you—*free !*"

She gazed down upon him without a word,
powerless to loose herself from his embrace,
and he, looking up at her, through all the
confusion of brain and heart that possessed
him, instantly missed something out of that
childish face . . . . the beauty was still there,
but the radiant, joyous freshness, the guileless
innocence of sin and evil, that he had been so
fiercely desirous that she should retain, where
were they now ? Something had gone from
her . . . . something had come to her . . . . of
this he was certain, but—what ?

A kind of horror grew slowly in his eyes,
reflected perhaps from hers, for she feared
him ; then his glance went faltering down to
the hand upon which the plain gold wedding-
ring shone. . . . .

He withdrew his right arm from her waist,
and lifted this hand, turned it over, looked at
it on the other side, parted the third and

fourth fingers, as though to make sure that
the circlet was perfect, going through all this
slowly and carefully, much as a madman may
do who knows himself to be mad, yet is trying with all his might to follow out the one
solitary thought that he equally knows to be
rational . . . . then, still holding her hand,
he looked up piteously, unsteadily, into
the girl's face, then down again at her
fingers. . . . .

"*Stolen!*" he said in a whisper, "*stolen!*"
and fell forward like a dead man upon her
breast.

     *   *   *   *   *

When Adam entered the garden a few
seconds later in search of his wife, it was
to discover her leaning over an insensible
man, whose arms were locked around her
while her fair hair mingled with his, as
she gazed into the face that lay upon her
bosom.

He stood still for a moment, his sight going
from him, his brain on fire, then he went on
again.

"He is dead!" said Mignon, lifting a cheek as pale and wan as the one that lay beneath her own.

"Mignon . . . ." said Adam, scarcely knowing what he said, the agony of his heart making his voice harsh and abrupt, "take your arms away from that man . . . . I command you not to touch him!"

A vain command! when she was powerless to free herself from that death-like, nerveless body, those heavy, clinging arms!

She strove to rise, but could not.

Adam drew Rideout's arms away, and made a gesture to Prue, who had followed him into the garden, to take Mignon's place.

"You will attend to this man," he said, "and use every means to restore him. Should you require other assistance, you will summon it, but he has merely fainted."

Then he turned to Mignon and took her hand in his. "Come!" he said.

"And leave him like that?" she cried in amazement. "Oh! how can you think of such a thing? Why, he may be *dead!*"

19—2

The hand that held hers closed so tightly and suddenly upon it, that she almost cried aloud for the pain, and yet he was not conscious of using any force or roughness, there was not one fibre of unmanliness or cruelty in him, but he was for the moment utterly maddened, and taken out of himself. . . . .

" Come !" he said quietly.

She caught her breath hard and looked up into his face, so youthful in its set calmness, and bearing in its clearly-cut features and firm square jaw, such ample indications of will and determination, then she wrenched her hand out of his, and flinging both her arms round Prue's neck, cried, through a rain of passionate tears, " I will stay with you—with you !— and oh! how I wish with all my heart and soul that I had never got married to-day !"

Some of those scalding tears splashed heavily downwards upon the weary care-worn face resting against Prue's shoulder, but he neither stirred nor spoke, the stupor of utter exhaustion was upon him and bound him hand and foot.

"Come!" said Adam for the third time, but, as he spoke, the fury of the tempest being now over, it flashed through his memory how only two nights ago he had sworn to her to be kind to her always . . . . to be *gentle* with her . . . . and this was the fulfilment of his vow!

"Take care of him, Prue," said Mignon, as she gave Prue a last frantic hug. "Poor fellow—poor *fellow!* And be sure and tell him that I *wanted* to wait until he was better, but that *he* would not let me."

"There," said Prue in a whisper, as the girl still clung to her, "go now, dear heart, your husband's waiting for you—your husband as loves you dearly, and him as you've sworn to honour and obey . . . . but come back to me soon, my heart, for it's sad I shall be without you, though never fear but I'll keep good watch for *her*, so don't fret yourself about that." . . . .

Why did the girl still pause to look down

long and wistfully at the face of the man to whom she had written her first love-letter, and whose looks she had never liked when he was strong, and bold, and gay ? Why did she, turning often, sobbing bitterly, as she went along the path by her husband's side, even pausing at the door that he held open for her, stand for some seconds, still looking back ? Then the door closed . . . . and the last page in the first volume of the book of Mignon's life was turned down for ever.

.

END OF VOL. I.

BILLING AND SONS, PRINTERS, GUILDFORD, SURREY.

S. & H.

www.ingramcontent.com/pod-product-compliance
Lightning Source LLC
Chambersburg PA
CBHW020844020726
47497CB00005B/1249